A Noble PURPOSE

CORNERSTONE SERIES | *Book 1*

LAURIE LUCKING

BELLATOR LUX

A Noble
PURPOSE

Contents

Dedication

For Nate – helpful, caring, honest, and so creative.
I so enjoyed hearing your insights on this book and look forward to brainstorming many more stories together!

Chapter 1

"Joyous twelvemonth, dear Verena. Joyous twelvemonth to you!"

I added an exaggerated vibrato on the last note as an extra tribute to my older sister on the anniversary of her birth, but of course she didn't smile. As far as I'd seen, her lips had barely twitched upward in years.

Verena nodded her acknowledgment. "Thank you." Her gaze drooped back to the generous slice of raspberry strudel on her glossy porcelain plate.

My lady's maid, Nadette, fluttered to my side and filled my teacup with steaming amber liquid. Biting her lip, she surreptitiously tucked a stray lock of dark hair into my chignon before backing her petite frame away from the table.

"I'm so glad your favorite dessert happens to be the same as mine." I raised a forkful of strudel toward Verena, as though in a toast.

"It is delicious." She nodded, her expression more suited to a funeral than a celebration in her honor.

Pappa gave Mamma a meaningful look, and I paused mid-bite. He'd been watching Verena in growing agitation for weeks, not that she seemed to notice. But from the intensity of his pacing every time he'd studied her with that determined set of his jaw, he had to be planning something.

Something Verena would absolutely hate, if I had to guess.

Mamma's eyes narrowed as she gave her head a tiny shake, but Pappa stared her down with furrowed brows. Eventually she sighed, giving her dainty lace-bordered napkin an irritated snap as she returned it to the table.

A glance at Verena confirmed she'd missed the entire exchange, distracted with slicing her pastry into precise squares before taking polite bites.

I was already scraping the last smear of raspberry jam from my plate's scalloped edge.

"Verena." Pappa's commanding tone didn't bode well. He let his fork drop with a clatter.

She flinched and looked up. "Yes?"

"This has gone on long enough." He gestured across the table at her.

"Luncheon?" She widened her deep brown eyes—the same shade as mine and Mamma's—in a melancholy query.

I dabbed my mouth to cover a giggle. *Oh, Verena.* For all her intelligence and training, she often failed to note the mood shifts taking place around her.

Pappa gave a blustery cough. "Luncheon? No, I mean this entire attitude of yours. You are the Crown Princess of Walthar, for heaven's sake, yet you mope around like a deprived child. You have every advantage, every luxury, and you can't even be bothered to smile."

All traces of humor fled as Verena's expression changed from bland indifference to sadness. *Don't be too hard on her, Pappa.*

"It's not that I'm ungrateful, Pappa. Truly. I apologize if my behavior shames you. I try to fulfill my duties as Crown Princess, even if I can't force a cheerful demeanor." An unusual hardness edged Verena's tone.

"Except you don't." Pappa rose from his chair, replacing it with a clatter. *Time for more pacing.* "You're turning 25 years old today, Verena. Yet you've hardly spoken a word to any of the local noblemen or visiting royalty. Have you no plans to marry and produce an heir?"

If possible, Verena's shoulders sagged further.

I squeezed her hand under the table, and she clutched my fingers like a lifeline. "That's not true, Pappa. Verena was downright chatty with the Earl of Arvid last month."

Mamma directed a gentle smile my way. "The Earl of Arvid is married, Liesel."

"What?" I flicked my free hand in a dramatic wave. "How very inconvenient. Perhaps he has a brother? Or cousin?"

"There's no need for matchmaking." Verena acknowledged my feeble attempt before turning back to Pappa. "I have little interest in romance, Pappa. Surely, I can rule just fine on my own."

"With my help, of course." I bounced in my seat. "And in my first step toward becoming a royal advisor, I really must insist you finish your strudel, Pappa. I believe it is the finest Cook has made yet."

Mamma nodded, flashing me a conspiratorial wink. "She'll likely be offended if you send it back to the kitchens uneaten. Perhaps this conversation can wait for another time."

The tightness in Pappa's jaw eased, and he rejoined us at the table. "We'd never want to offend dear Cook. But I'm afraid this conversation can't wait." His gaze hardened as he turned back to Verena. "What is this about ruling alone? What about heirs to the royal line? A family? It seems matchmaking will become necessary, Verena, if you fail to find a future king on your own."

"If you wish, Pappa." Verena glanced to the tall window as her throat convulsed in a hard swallow. "But if this is about smiling more, I will try harder to appear more grateful for—"

"No." Pappa's fist collided with the polished arm of his chair. "No, that's not enough."

Mamma squeezed his shoulder. "I think what your father is tryin' to say is that we wish for you to find true happiness, not just the appearance of it."

"Precisely." He patted Mamma's hand. "But I'm at a loss as to how to accomplish that, aside from finding a man who can bring you joy where the rest of us have failed."

I leaned forward. "But if Verena doesn't want a husband, maybe a puppy could cheer her up instead. Or..."

Pappa silenced me with a look, his expression both fond and exasperated.

Mamma covered her mouth with her napkin, her cough sounding suspiciously like a giggle.

"I am quite determined. Something must be done, and I hope in time you'll thank us." Pappa stood again, regal in a silver-edged vest that matched his closely-cropped hair. "At tonight's celebration ball, we'll make a special announcement. A challenge, you might say." He raised a fist, as though practicing for the evening's event. "The first man who can make you laugh—truly laugh with real pleasure—shall earn your hand in marriage."

"Verena, wait!" I chased my sister's retreating form down the wide castle corridor. Thick, elaborate rugs dampened my hurried steps—thank the snows, since I'd never avoid a lecture on proper decorum if Mamma or Nadette heard me clomping through the hall.

My sister had seemed to fold in on herself after Pappa's proclamation, his every detail—from the trumpet blare that would announce a new suitor to the sikha juice that would mark the back of each unsuccessful gentleman's hand to prevent repeated attempts—making her retreat further.

A flower preparing its delicate petals for a storm.

But no matter how many quips I made about a clownish future king, Pappa had failed to relent. Failed to see how his scheme could be anything but the perfect solution to both Verena's unmarried state and her future happiness.

I caught up with Verena and grasped her shoulder. "I can tell you hate this plan. And I don't blame you. But Pappa hasn't made the announcement yet, and I don't believe Mamma likes this any more than we do. We still have time to devise our own proposal before the ball tonight and convince him—"

"No, Liesel." She halted and faced me, sorrow radiating from her entire being. "I have embarrassed our family and made everyone who interacts with us think less of the Waltharian royal line."

I pressed her upper arms. "That's not true. Pappa can get a bit dramatic about our family pride, but—"

"In this case, I imagine he's right." She held up her hand. "Thank you for wanting to help. For wanting to defend me, though I hardly deserve it."

I stroked my thumbs on the silky sleeves of her pale blue day dress but held my tongue.

"I've never been lighthearted, like you. I don't know how to make myself cheerful, or to even pretend. Especially after..." She heaved a sigh.

After what? "Verena, did something happen? Did someone hurt you, or insult you, or..." My mind raced through dozens of possibilities, my anger flaring at anyone who would dare add to my vulnerable sister's sadness.

"No, nothing like that." Verena's head shake swung her chocolate-brown curls in a slow cadence. Glancing up and down the hall, she tugged me toward the nearest door frame. "It's just harder than ever to act carefree as more of the weight of the kingdom gets placed on my shoulders."

"I understand." I quirked a grin. "Though even before you could comprehend the concept of being the Crown Princess, I'm not sure anyone would've described you as *carefree*."

"True." The corners of her full lips curved slightly less downward, the closest thing to a smile I could hope for.

While I didn't agree with his methods, I could understand Pappa's desperate desire to put a genuine smile on my sister's face. "Do you need me to take on some of your responsibilities? Or perhaps I could plan an excursion for us? I've heard the southern provinces are beautiful in the spring. I still think Pappa might relent if we come up with a promising alternative."

"I doubt any number of excursions could change how the Holy One formed my heart and mind. And I don't mind the responsibilities. The welfare of our kingdom means a great deal to me." She leaned against the wall, running the golden chain of her necklace through her fingers. "So if Pappa thinks this plan will improve how I'm perceived—redeem some of our family's honor, somehow—then I owe it to him to give it a try."

If only Pappa could value Verena's compassion, patience, and loyalty instead of viewing her disposition as a problem to be fixed. "Well, if you're determined to go through with this, then I'll be at your side. I'll sit with you on that balcony watching every suitor, and I'll even try to hold back my laughter for every man who fails to entertain you."

Verena patted my hand. "I hope you know that your support—your willingness to listen and at least try to understand, despite our differences—does make me happy. It's good to know I'm not alone. That not everyone thinks I'm just ridiculous or over-dramatic."

"Not at all. You feel things deeply. You take on everyone else's cares as your own. You refuse to pretend to feel something you don't. There's no shame or embarrassment in that." I twined my arm through hers as we started back down the hall. "Now we just need to find a man who can see you in the same light. And hopefully make you laugh on occasion, as well."

Verena didn't respond, keeping her gaze fixed on the floor.

Pappa, what are you getting her into?

"I actually found that one rather amusing." I nudged Verena's side as we retreated from her balcony back into her chambers. "And he was young, not too painful to look at."

Verena sighed as she closed the door behind us, shutting out the cool, humid breeze. "I didn't notice."

Something between despair and anger flared in my chest. Pappa's proclamation had been met with enthusiasm by everyone, with the exception of Verena. Amateur jugglers and acrobats, shy gentlemen telling well-known jokes, jolly orators with booming laughs—today's suitor was the latest in an endless series of failed attempts from commoners and noblemen alike to entertain my sister and the crowd that assembled each time the trumpet blared. His ability to mimic voices from a harsh schoolmaster to an exhausted matron to a lispy child had produced many chuckles from the onlookers.

But not even a trace of a smile from my sister.

My exasperation broke free in a huff. "Why would you fail to notice such a thing, Verena? When the poor man was out there making himself look ridiculous for you? In order to become your husband!"

"In order to become the king." A hint of fire simmered behind her eyes. She lowered into an armchair and picked up her embroidery, facing away from me.

"Not necessarily." I tried to gentle my tone. "Verena, have you considered that some of these men might find you attractive or intriguing? Might want to make you laugh not for the position but because they want to make you happy? It's not fair to dismiss each one before they've even had a chance to impress you."

She shrugged. "That may be true. But it's also not fair to give false hope to any of these gentlemen when I have no wish to marry." Her needle stabbed through the cloth as though it were the cause of her woes.

"No matter how reluctantly, you did agree to Pappa's plan." I grasped the dark green folds of my chiffon skirt to hide my clenched fists. "It's hardly cooperating if you're not actually looking for a husband among these suitors."

Her posture stiffened. "I appear on my balcony each time that trumpet blares and politely watch every performance. I'm fulfilling precisely the terms I agreed to."

Rubbing my temple, I replayed her words in my mind. "You truly have no desire to marry? Ever?"

"I'd rather not talk about it." She twisted to an awkward angle in her chair in an unsuccessful attempt to hide her face.

You won't get rid of me that easily. I sprawled comfortably on the settee on the other side of her marble fireplace. "I assumed it would be nice for you to have a husband one day. Someone to talk to, be affectionate with. Someone to help so you don't have to rule the kingdom alone."

She tipped her head against the cushion of her chair. "Perhaps. But I could hardly make a decision to marry based merely on *that*." She flicked her hand toward the balcony with a sniff.

"I understand." I ran my fingers across the soft velvet fabric draped over the armrest. "Is there someone you *would* want to marry? Pappa might be willing to call this whole thing off if he knew a gentleman had already caught your fancy. Or perhaps the man you care for will come try his hand at making you laugh."

She set her jaw, but something shimmered suspiciously close to her eye. Was Verena...crying?

Keeping my movements slow and non-threatening, I approached her chair and knelt by her feet. "Verena, you used to smile. To laugh. At least a little. I remember, back when I wished I could be beautiful and grown-up like you instead of an awkward girl. What happened? If you're certain no potential husband could bring a smile back to your face, then what could?"

Verena set aside her embroidery, pressing her fingers over her eyes. "There was one gentleman who could always make me laugh. But he's long gone."

I sat up, mind reeling. Verena had been in love? Had he jilted or disappointed her, or...? I kept my voice low, the tone I'd use to calm a jittery elk. "Who was he?"

Her snort could've almost passed for a bitter laugh. "You'd think me foolish."

"I doubt it."

She swallowed, keeping her gaze on the floor. "Pappa and Mamma certainly would've never approved."

I picked at a fuzz on the rug, hoping the distracted gesture hid my whirling thoughts. "Did they know about him?"

"They knew of him, but never that I..." She shook her head. "It hardly mattered, since he didn't reciprocate."

Sweet Verena. I wanted to hug her, but I kept my spot on the floor. "But you said they wouldn't approve. So is it possible he returned your feelings but didn't feel free to voice them?"

"Either way, I'll never see him again." A hopeless shrug drooped her shoulders.

I placed a hand on her knee. I almost didn't want to know, but... "Did he die?"

Her leg jerked. "What? No. At least, I certainly hope not. He was sent away."

"Oh." Relieved, my mind returned to its puzzling. "But I thought you said Pappa and Mamma didn't know about how you...the way you felt about him."

She finally met my eyes with an expression of resignation. "You aren't going to let this rest, are you?"

"Not if it could hold a key to your future happiness."

"Fine." She threaded her fingers together, color rising up her neck. "Do you remember my former guard, Sir Jonas?"

"Sir Jonas." I let the name linger, trying to picture a face.

"Good-natured, quick to smile. But quite...clumsy." Now her cheeks resembled ripening tomatoes.

"Yes!" I bounced on my knees. "I liked that one. He always gave me peppermints when Mamma and Pappa weren't looking."

"That sounds like him." She wrung her hands in her lap. "Well, I became very fond of Sir Jonas. He was never as stiff and formal as everyone else around the castle. He always went out of his way to make me smile. And he listened. Even though I was several years younger, he thought what I had to say was important. At least, he acted like it. He didn't think I was silly for being sad when the most beautiful autumn leaves detached from their branches or when a piece of music in a minor key put me in a melancholy mood all afternoon."

Someone who didn't roll his eyes at Verena's moods or dismiss her as melodramatic? "No wonder you fell in love with him."

Her eyes widened. "Fell in love with...?" She slumped back in her chair. "I suppose I did. After he was sent away, it's just never been the same."

"But I still don't understand *why* he was sent away."

She massaged her forehead. "For all his wonderful qualities, Sir Jonas wasn't much of a knight. The poor man seemed to injure himself or someone else every time he tried to wield a sword. After years of little improvement, Pappa declared him an embarrassment to the castle guard and sent him away."

"Oh, Verena. I had no idea." Rising to a crouch, I placed an arm around her shoulders.

She squeezed my hand. "Of course you didn't. I was eighteen at the time, so you would've been, what...twelve? Hardly an age to entrust you with my romantic woes."

"True. Though I'm sorry I didn't notice, all the same." I leaned my head against her arm. "But you think he didn't return your feelings? It sounds to me like he cared for you a great deal."

"I believe he did, in his way." Her lips rose into what could almost be called a fond smile. "But as a young girl he enjoyed entertaining, or perhaps a little sister. Nothing romantic."

"Hmm, maybe at the time. But that was seven years ago! Though you may be oblivious, I've seen the way men look at you these days. I'm certain you would catch his eye." I bobbed on the balls of my feet. "If only he knew about Pappa's declaration, he could come back and be the one to make you laugh."

"If only." Her sigh was half wistful, half resigned. "But he could hardly be expected to return of his own volition when he was sent away for being an inept knight."

My shoulders sagged. *Fair point.*

"Besides, I doubt he'd even hear about the proclamation. He was sent all the way to Ormande."

Chapter 2

ORMANDE. THE NAME HAD nudged at my thoughts ever since Verena had first named it a week before. I'd stopped in the library to verify the province's location, and it was as far into the mountain range to the north as I'd thought.

As I'd feared.

Verena was right to assume little news traveled that far afield from Telynn Castle. Five days' ride from here, at least. And not easy terrain, if the jagged points on the map representing the Norden Mountains were any indication. But a few paths cut through the mountain range, mostly running parallel to the streams that meandered across each ridge and valley, and an occasional village or estate provided scattered dots of civilization.

A difficult area to traverse, but apparently not impossible.

I sagged onto the hard stone bench on Verena's balcony, releasing a sigh. The bugle had sounded minutes before, the third time this week. The initial deluge of suitors had trickled to a steady stream in the month since

Pappa's announcement, but it seemed the supply of hopeful would-be kings wasn't going to subside anytime soon.

Verena turned to me, her eyes narrowed in concern. "I appreciate your support in this, Liesel. Truly. But while I have no choice in the matter, you do. I don't want to cause you suffering. There's no need for both of us to sit through these demonstrations day after day."

I opened my mouth to reassure her that I wouldn't leave her side throughout this process. Then I closed it again. Aside from offering sisterly support on this balcony, I was accomplishing nothing by staying at the castle, watching her grow more miserable—and Pappa more frustrated—with each gentleman's failed attempt.

If Sir Jonas would never hear news of the proclamation out in Ormande, never be presumptuous enough to return to the castle on his own... Could I be brave enough to seek him out? Convince him to come back myself?

I blinked, suddenly aware of Verena's continued scrutiny. A practiced smile rose to my lips. "Perhaps you're right. Much as I hate the thought of leaving you to bear this alone, I have been feeling quite restless. Would you be upset with me if I ran off for a few weeks to visit Lady Ethelde?" I rattled off the first friend's name that came to mind. One who lived far enough to justify a longer trip.

"Not in the slightest." She patted my hand. "I'll miss you, of course, but it would bring me comfort to know you're no longer putting your own life on hold for my sake."

"Thank you." I squeezed her fingers. "I shall speak to Mamma about it."

The trumpet blared a second time, and the crowd parted for a lanky man strutting through the courtyard. I scooted forward on the bench.

Another man in a mask. This was the fourth suitor who wore a black mask across his eyes and nose, as though attending a masquerade ball. The clothing varied, but each had a similar build, the same short dark hair... I squinted at his hands but could detect no remnant of sikha juice.

Did the same man keep returning? Each failed suitor was marched to one of the kitchen maids to receive a tattoo painted with sikha berry juice on the back of his hand. A mark that should've lasted six months at least. Had someone found a way to remove the stain so quickly?

I leaned forward, attempting to view the man in as much detail as possible. The set of his mouth was different from the masked suitor of a few days before, as was his posture. *Not the same man, then.* But could it be pure coincidence that so many similar-looking men had each chosen to wear a mask?

Theories prodded the corners of my mind like the birds that accidentally found themselves trapped in our elk barns. I blinked and rubbed the crease from my forehead as the suitor strode forward, his gaze on our balcony.

"Fair Princess Verena. I am grateful beyond measure to have the opportunity to press my suit to you today. I'm afraid my background doesn't lend itself well to comedic endeavors, but I will do what I can with my training in palace defense."

His confident words held a slight accent. Markan, perhaps? With a salute, he straightened and clicked his heels together. "Forward, MARCH."

The crowd parted as he proceeded to our right with exaggerated steps. "Face right." He veered right again just as he reached the waist-high wall that sectioned off the outer courtyard.

"Pardon me." He marched through a flock of giggling young ladies, his steps higher and faster than before. His knees practically bumped his chin as he pranced past, following the orders of his own commands.

My eyes wandered to Verena, who watched the man's antics with an expression of respect. Not a flicker of amusement. Considering the oddity of the mask, I would've hardly encouraged her to embrace this particular man's suit, anyway. But how long could this charade continue? Pappa's assertion that it would help Verena's reputation rested fully on her choosing a husband from among these suitors. And then being happier as a result of that choice.

If Verena was already in love, she'd never choose one of these men. At least, not willingly. Which would only make her seem more fickle and capricious than ever. Making Pappa more angry, and Verena more penitent...

I suppressed a groan as the suitor weaved his way between onlookers in a complex series of maneuvers. If only Pappa realized that the best way he could support Verena's happiness was to embrace the serious, contemplative young lady she was instead of bemoaning the gregarious socialite she'd never be.

"Don't you think it's odd?" My personal guard, Sir Albrecht, was unnecessarily escorting me to my chambers following dinner that evening.

He kept his face forward, his posture stiff as though he hadn't heard me. *Typical.* Though he couldn't be more than four years my senior, Sir Albrecht was as dour as the white-haired curmudgeons who served on Pappa's council.

I poked his arm. "Sir Albrecht, you know I refuse to pretend you don't exist. So I'll say again... Don't you think it's odd?" I glanced up and down the empty corridor and lowered my voice. "About my sister's latest suitor."

He tilted his head with a raised brow. "Do I find it odd that gentlemen are lining up to embarrass themselves in front of Princess Verena? That the most ridiculous of them all will marry her and become the next King of Walthar?"

I rubbed my temple with a sigh. "Perhaps pretending you don't exist would serve me better, after all. But while Pappa's contest for Verena's hand is a bit…unusual…I was referring to the masked suitor this afternoon. He's the fourth one to wear a mask."

Sir Albrecht shrugged and resumed walking, his tall black boots clicking a steady rhythm. "The types of gentlemen who would attempt this kind of task are likely to be swayed by whatever they think might be considered the height of fashion. And I certainly wouldn't blame them for wanting to hide their identity in an attempt to minimize their embarrassment."

I hustled to keep up with his faster pace. "It's a fair point, but I can't help thinking there's more to it than that. Each of the masked men has been tall and thin with short, dark hair."

His lips rose in a smirk. "Paying close attention to your sister's suitors, hmm? Perhaps hoping to choose from among her rejections?"

My dignified cough came out as more of a strangled snort. "Hardly. I tend to prefer men with longer hair." I refused to glance toward his light brown hair, which unfortunately fell in quite attractive waves just beyond his ears. "More importantly, I'd never take advantage of my sister's ordeal. I've paid attention to the masked men specifically because it's such a strange commonality." My heart pumped a little faster at the prospect of revealing my new theory. "The one today had a Markan accent, and it occurred to me that they've all borne a resemblance to Prince Carre of Markou. His father has been trying to negotiate an alliance with Walthar for years. What if he's trying to use Pappa's challenge to marry Verena?"

Sir Albrecht frowned. "Surely they can't all be him. Sir Ennoh checks carefully for traces of sikha juice. Masks may be allowed, but not gloves."

"Exactly. They're not all the same person, and I don't believe any of them were the prince himself. Hence the masks." I chewed on my lip. "But what if he sent all the masked suitors? If they each look similar to Prince Carre, he may try to claim credit if one of them makes Verena laugh."

He scratched at the scruff shadowing his jaw. "It's an interesting theory. But why would he need to go to such lengths to secure an alliance? What is your father's objection?"

I tamped down a smile. This was why I'd consulted Sir Albrecht. *Reluctantly.* Despite his gruffness, his mind was sharp and strategic. "Let's just say Markou isn't known for its fidelity in alliances. Nor are the men of the Markan royal line known for their fidelity in marriages." I grimaced. It was the most accurate way to describe Prince Carre and his father without using language unfit for a princess.

"I see." He darted me a sideways glance. "Have you alerted your sister or parents to your suspicions?"

"No." I tugged at the lacy cuff of my sleeve, looking forward to the soft fabric of my nightdress. "Pappa has been so tense lately, and Verena detests all this attention and pageantry enough already without adding the possibility of an underhanded scheme."

Sir Albrecht leaned a hand against the wall when we arrived at my door, his thumb brushing the golden edge of a tapestry depicting two elk facing off with intertwined antlers. "This isn't likely to end anytime soon, then, is it? If your sister doesn't like this method of choosing a husband, but your father wants to insist?"

"I wish I could disagree, but it's an accurate assessment." My heavy exhale fluttered the dark curls that had escaped my braid.

He shrugged. "Then maybe it doesn't matter. The mystery of the masked men, that is. If Princess Verena has no intention of choosing a husband from among her suitors, then the Markan plot—if such a plot exists—is doomed to failure."

"Perhaps." I crossed my arms over my chest. "But I still don't like the thought of so many of Prince Carre's men lurking about Telynn Castle. Please pay extra attention to the masked suitors, just in case."

"Of course. Though your worries are likely unfounded." His lips quirked into a lopsided smile that transformed him from curmudgeon to mischievous lad. "I somehow doubt they'll manage to catch your sister off-guard with a surprise laugh, no matter how many suitors they send."

"That's true enough." I returned his smile with my own, chagrined that *Sir Albrecht* was the one bringing levity to the conversation. "Are you certain you don't want to put yourself in the role of suitor? After all, you'd find Verena far easier to look after than me. She doesn't talk as much and gets into far less trouble."

He released a half-scoff, half-chuckle. "Now that I would believe. But I wouldn't have the first idea how to make your sister laugh, and I've no intention of humiliating myself in front of such a crowd."

My grin turned sly. "I hear masks are all the rage..."

He shook his head. "I came to Telynn Castle to serve as a knight, not to marry a princess." He glanced out the nearest window, where twilight was fading to a deep, inky blue. "And as your assigned guard, I should encourage you to retire for the evening."

"Hmph, you're no better than Nadette." My lady's maid might smile more than Sir Albrecht, but she was just as fond of rules and propriety.

He raised his hands in feigned innocence. "If you weren't so sorely in need of our wisdom, we wouldn't feel compelled to share it on such a regular basis."

"Aren't I a lucky one?" I rolled my eyes at him. "I bid thee goodnight, oh wise one."

He bowed. "Goodnight, my unwilling pupil."

I ducked into my chambers with a laugh and closed the door behind me. Light flickered from evenly-spaced wall sconces, casting my writing desk and bookshelf into murky shadows. I crossed to my bedchamber, where Nadette had already laid a pale pink nightdress across my coverlet. No doubt she'd return soon to help me unfasten the pearl buttons lining the back of my dress.

Stomach churning, I picked up the novel from my bedside table.

If Prince Carre had set his sights on Verena's hand in marriage, would he let his failure to make her laugh stop him? How many more potential suitors would he send before he lost his patience?

I sank into a chair by the fireplace, the book unopened in my lap. Could I thwart whatever might be the next step in his plans?

Resolve settled in my chest, heavy but exhilarating. Verena's Sir Jonas had to be out there somewhere. For her sake—and for the sake of keeping Walthar out of the clutches of Markou and Prince Carre—I had to find him.

Chapter 3

Guilt gnawed at my midsection as I made my way to the training grounds. Even with her blessing, I hated to abandon Verena when she was the subject of so much gossip and attention. And sneaking off to find Sir Jonas would require so much deception...

Not that it would be my first scheme that involved hiding certain key pieces of information from my overprotective parents and guards, but I still didn't relish the thought.

I tightened my fingers around the handle of the willow basket I carried as the log fencing surrounding the barracks came into view. There was no point in planning further for an excursion to seek out Sir Jonas until I knew for certain where he was. If he really had been sent to Ormande, then Sir Ennoh, the Captain of the Guard, would be the most likely to know.

But how to wheedle the information from him without rousing suspicion...

"Look sharp, Nefen. No foe on the battlefield'll wait for you to fix your bloomin' hair before they run you through." Sir Ennoh's gruff voice barreled across the training yard. "He's givin' you an opening, Nefen. Best take it." He shook his head, softening to a grumble. "If he paid more attention to 'is opponent than the young ladies watchin' the bout, he'd have been the victor five times over by now. Ne'er seen such a dandy."

The referenced young ladies—a set of three who seemed to follow Sir Nefen wherever he sauntered—squealed as their hero narrowly dodged a blow.

Skirting around them, I sidled up to Sir Ennoh and cleared my throat.

Sir Ennoh rounded on me, his grizzled brows raised. "Why, Princess Liesel! Good to see you, lass. What brings you to the trainin' grounds today? Not that popinjay Sir Nefen, I hope."

Laughing, I leaned close to conspiratorially whisper, "I haven't the least interest in Sir Nefen. He has enough young ladies vying for his attention without adding me to the mix. I'm here to see you, of course. I can think of no one better to share my picnic lunch."

His loud chuckle startled the nearest guards watching the sword fight. "Ah, you're far too kind to an old man. But I'll take you up on your offer, all the same." He turned back to the knights under his command. "Take a break, lads. Go see if Cook has luncheon ready for you. But no combin' that hair o' yours, Nefen, you hear me?"

The knight in question scowled but nodded.

"There's times for a knight to be spic and span, and times for 'im to focus on the task at hand. That boy'd best learn the difference." He patted my arm. "Not that I should be too hard on the lads, wantin' to look their best with the fair Princess Liesel about."

I giggled. "An excess of vanity is not an attractive trait, so you're quite right to correct him."

"Where's your Albrecht?" He glanced behind us, a scowl returning to his weathered face.

Hardly *my* Albrecht. "Hopefully having lunch like I told him to. I assured him I'd be plenty safe in your company." Sir Ennoh had been among the retinue that accompanied Mamma to Walthar for her betrothal and marriage. A skilled knight, as well as a fatherly figure for Mamma in her new home, he'd quickly risen through the ranks until he was overseeing all the castle guards.

Ennoh grunted. "I'd protect you with my life, and that's a fact. But he'd better not've taken you at your word. I know there's a bit of mischief in my favorite lass."

"He'd say far more than a *bit*. But he shadows me everywhere, don't you worry." I squinted up at him. "And I've never once seen him fussing with his hair."

He barked a laugh. "Now, there's a good lad."

The ground squished beneath my half boots as we reached a clearing with several large rocks. I wrinkled my nose at the mud as I assumed my usual spot, but at least the ice had melted.

I passed Ennoh a meat-filled pastry. "Aside from vain Sir Nefen, do you have a promising group of recruits?"

"How you spoil me." He raised his pastry with a nod of thanks. "Good-hearted boys, on the whole. Never seem to be as tough as they used to, but p'raps that's just my old age talkin'. Hopefully they'll never have to see a war. At least, as long as that King of Markou behaves 'imself."

"What a blessing that would be." I picked off a bite of flaky crust, aiming to look pensive. "Do you ever get knights who don't work out? How do you handle it?"

"On occasion." He leaned back against a rough tree trunk. "How it's handled depends on the problem. If a man proves untrustworthy—untrue to the crown—he gets sent away right quick. Time for 'im to find a new profession, since he won't be gettin' a letter of recommendation from us."

"That makes sense. Is that the only reason knights get sent away?" I tilted my head in innocent inquiry.

Ennoh swiped a hand over his mouth. "Usually. If the man's loyal, we try our best to work with 'im. But there're a few even I can't train." He huffed a laugh. "Few years back, there was a knight as honest as they come. Poor man couldn't wield a weapon if 'is ma's life depended on it. Finally had to send 'im off, though it pained me to do it. As much for 'is own sake as ours."

"Oh dear, that does sound difficult." I dug in the picnic basket, though the napkin I sought was on top. "Did he get sent away the same as the others?"

He shook his head and took a swig from his water flask. "Nah, couldn't do that to the boy. Hard enough on 'is pride as it was. Made some inquiries, found a position for 'im off in Ormande."

I held back a wince. So he really had been sent that far away. "But what could he do in Ormande that he couldn't do here?"

Ennoh accepted the napkin piled with cloudberries I passed to him. "That was the beauty of it. His Majesty values me for more than my brawn, you know." He tapped his thinning gray hair with a wink.

I nodded and gave an encouraging smile. Words might distract him from his story.

"Lord Hamelun out in that direction needs a great many guards on account of his large property stretchin' across the mountainside. Mostly just marchin' the perimeter, raisin' the alarm if a predator's spotted."

I popped a berry into my mouth, chewing slowly as the tangy juice burst on my tongue. "Ah, so he still got to be a knight?"

"In a manner o' speakin'." He wiped purple drips from his fingers. "Seemed to be workin' out well when he first got there, and I haven't heard anythin' since. I'd imagine he's settled in nicely. Always was a hard-workin' fellow."

"I hope so." My mind whirled as my gaze wandered to the trees, their branches tipped with hopeful green buds. Verena hadn't been mistaken about Ormande, and now I had Lord Hamelun's name to work with.

Sir Ennoh sat up, giving his closely-cropped beard a tug. "But enough about my men. Let's hear 'bout life in the castle. Has your sister taken a shine to any of those jesters tryin' to make her laugh?"

I forced my smile to stay in place. "Not yet."

And she likely never would, unless I could make my way up to Ormande.

"Mamma?" I tapped on the mahogany door to my mother's parlor, which she'd left ajar.

"Liesel." Her face brightened, revealing the sparkling, dimpled smile that had caught Pappa's eye back when the Joran royal family had visited Telynn Castle. "Do come in."

I chose a seat near the fireplace's cozy glow as she placed her quill back in its silver stand.

"I thought you'd be outside on such a delightful day." She rose, straightening her amethyst brocade skirt. "Spring is arriving at last."

I tucked my legs beneath me. "I just came from a picnic with Ennoh at the training grounds. The sunshine does feel lovely, though there's a chill in the breeze."

"That mountain air." She took the chair across from me. Her dark hair, lightened at the temples with hints of gray, crowned her head in a thick braid. "A visit to Ennoh, did you say? I'm sure he was thrilled."

"He never turns down the offer of a picnic." I grinned, picturing the relief on the faces of his would-be knights. "It gives his poor trainees a bit of a break, if nothing else."

She chuckled. "There's no one as disciplined as Sir Ennoh. Your father will be at a loss to find 'is replacement someday." She leaned forward, her hands clasped under her chin. "And now you thought to similarly brighten my day?"

I swallowed. "You know I always wish to brighten your day, Mamma. But I must confess, I—"

Mamma's vibrant laugh cut me off. "I could tell somethin' more specific brought you to my door, and I won't hold it against you. What's on your mind, my dear?"

I turned my gaze to the dancing flames. Why did I never take the time to plan out this type of request ahead of time? "I—I've found myself a bit restless the past few days. Perhaps it's that feeling of spring in the air." Hopefully my smile looked chagrined rather than fake. "In any case, I thought an outing might do me good. Would it be any trouble for me to visit Lady Ethelde for a week or two?"

"Ah, my poor girl." Mamma patted my hand. "I don't wonder that this odd business with your sister has made you restless. So much pressure and attention on her. Gossip and speculation. Never knowin' when the next bugle call might invade your peace of mind and plans for the day. Your pappa and his ultimatums." She pinched the bridge of her nose. "It's enough to tempt me to escape for a bit of a holiday as well."

I nodded sympathetically, trying to keep the panic off my face. It hadn't occurred to me she might want to join my outing.

"You would be very much missed, but you've earned yourself a bit o' fun." She glanced to the door and lowered her voice. "I can't express what a blessing you are, Liesel. Cheerful, cooperative, always puttin' a smile on our faces."

The praise filled my heart with an odd mix of warmth and sadness. I knew how my parents appreciated my lively disposition and relied upon me to lighten tense moments within our family or when entertaining visitors.

What more could I ask than to be loved and appreciated by my family? And yet...at times I felt as trapped by my role as the cheerful princess as Verena seemed in hers as the miserable one.

"Thank you, Mamma." I shifted under her warm gaze. "But you know Verena does try, in her way. She just feels things so very deeply."

"Of course. I hope she values the loyal friend she has in you." She tweaked my chin before settling back against the pillows cushioning her chair. "Yes, Verena has a lot to offer the world if she would only open herself to those possibilities. I somehow doubt this contest is what she needed, but the Holy One can work in mysterious ways. And we're in the thick of it now, aren't we?"

"We certainly are." I shook my head, recalling the ridiculous marching and pivoting antics of the man from the day prior. "But you never know, someone may catch Verena's eye yet."

Mamma released a long sigh. "If he does, I can only hope he will make a decent king in the bargain." She blinked and flicked a loose thread from her sleeve. "But you came to ask about Lady Ethelde, and I think it's a lovely notion. A week or two, I believe you said? I'm sure we could spare the two-seated sled, or perhaps—"

"No need." The fewer people involved in my deception, the better. "I'd much rather ride, especially if the weather remains so favorable. You know how I enjoy long afternoons on Tassie, and Nadette has little Hilde."

"Your elk?" She gripped the arms of her chair. "Are you sure they could accomplish it in one day?"

"If the roads are clear. It would give us an excuse to ride fast. You know Tassie can keep up with any bull, and Hilde makes up in spirit what she lacks in height."

"My wild girl." Her soft smile radiated both caution and indulgence. "I suppose I don't mind if Nadette doesn't."

"It will give us the utmost flexibility to stay for as long or short a time as we like." Who knew how long it would actually take us to ride to Ormande and back, after all?

Poor Nadette would likely *not* be as enthusiastic about the plan as I made her sound. At least, not my actual plan. But for all her worries and reminders about manners and proper behavior, her devotion to me never failed. Much as she would balk at the idea of taking a multi-week trek to an unfamiliar part of the kingdom, she'd indulge me with enough convincing.

And maybe some cinnamon buns for good measure.

"True. I suppose the sled might get stuck in any number of ruts if the ground is muddy." Mamma traced a finger along the golden tassels of the nearest pillow. "Though you must also be accompanied by a guard, of course."

My attempt to turn my groan into a cough wasn't very convincing, if Mamma's amused expression was any indication. But I could only imagine the look on Sir Albrecht's face if he were to catch wind of my harebrained scheme.

She raised a hand. "I know how you cherish your freedom, Liesel, but we can't have you beset by thieves or bandits along the way."

I tapped my toes inside my slipper. "Fine. But can he just accompany us there and then return? Sir Albrecht would never forgive me if I took him away from his training for weeks at a time, just to watch me drink tea and wander Lady Ethelde's gardens."

She tilted her head, delicate brows raised. "Sir Albrecht's top priority must always be your safety, whether traipsin' across the country or sittin' at a tea party."

"I know, but..." *My plan can't possibly work if Sir Albrecht has to be involved.*

"He's only doin' his job, Liesel, though I know you find him to be a bit stifling." She regarded me over steepled fingers. "However, in this case, I acknowledge your point. When you write to Lady Ethelde, make sure to ask if they could spare a guard or two for your return trip."

"Of course." I lowered my head in a submissive pose, hiding a grin.

Hopefully it wouldn't be any trouble to shake Sir Albrecht on the day of our departure.

Chapter 4

WE BROKE FROM TREE cover into an open meadow. *On our way at last.* After days of packing and half-truths and two more suitors Verena suffered through without a hint of a smile, I was free.

Far behind us, the tallest spires of Telynn Castle peeked above the foliage. I twitched the reins of my mount, Tassie, slowing her to a halt. My favorite elk from our barns, she was tall for a female, with reddish-brown fur at her head and neck fading to tan at her back. Her sturdy legs and cloven hooves were a perfect combination for speed and navigating mountainous terrain.

But the mountains lay far ahead. Spring had painted the distant peaks in a breathtaking mix of vivid greens, pinks, and purples. Snow tipped each crest like a jagged white cap. I breathed deeply of the fresh air, not caring whether the hint of lilacs was real or imagined. The open, flat space leading to the foothills would provide the perfect opportunity to gain more distance from the castle and anyone who would disapprove of our quest.

"It is beautiful, milady." Nadette pulled her small elk, Hilde, to a stop at my side. "But couldn't we explore for the day and return by dusk? Or surely Lady Ethelde wouldn't mind a surprise visit, if you explained your letter had gone astray."

"No, Nadette." Shifting the reins to one hand, I patted my lady's maid's shoulder. Only five years my senior, she'd always felt almost as much a big sister to me as Verena. "I'm afraid, in this case, only Ormande will do. I truly believe the gentleman we're seeking will be the one to make my sister laugh." I'd disclosed the general nature of our excursion to her, leaving out the details Verena had shared about her affection for Sir Jonas.

"What a lovely outcome that would be." She turned to me, worrying her lower lip. "But are you sure it's worth the risk? Good gracious, your parents would dismiss me in a blink if they knew I was a part of this. And I'd never forgive myself if you were attacked by bandits or some wild mountain creature." Her voice lowered to a whisper, as though her words alone might wake a fearsome beast from miles away.

"We'll steer clear of wild creatures and bandits, and you know I'd never let you get sacked for something that was entirely my idea." I took in her tense posture, from her thin shoulders clad in a creamy wool shawl to her legs hugging Hilde's sides beneath a gray split skirt. "However, if you'd rather not accompany me, I do understand. You could spend a few weeks in the village while I—"

"Certainly not, milady." She shook her head, setting the blond wisps escaped from her bonnet dancing. "I'd never let you go alone. If you're that determined, then let's see this through." Her hands trembled, but she took a fortifying breath.

"Thank you." I squeezed her fingers, my spirits buoyant once more. While I'd never order Nadette to do something of this magnitude against her will, my trek would've been much more daunting—and far less pleasant—if I had to undertake it alone. "I'm very grateful to have you along. Just think of the adventures we'll have."

"Hopefully only agreeable ones." Gripping her reins, she gave me a tight smile. "We'd best continue, then."

"That's the spirit! We'll—"

The sound of pounding hoof beats interrupted my response. Nadette's gaze flew to mine, her green eyes wide.

"Princess Liesel! Wait!" The shout held a unique combination of confidence and annoyance that could only belong to Sir Albrecht.

Well, isn't that a soggy biscuit?

Pressing a finger to my temple, I turned Tassie in a half circle. With a reluctant nod, I gestured for Nadette to do the same.

Why, why, *why* did he have to find us? When we had already disappeared from sight of the castle?

"Sir Albrecht." Even I was tempted to shiver at the iciness of my tone. "Am I needed at home?"

"No, Princess." His narrowed gaze took in more details as he approached. "But where are you going?"

I held my shoulders stiff, my mind a cacophony of incomplete thoughts. I'd sent him on an errand for Sir Ennoh to avoid this very scenario. "I'm off on a visit to my friend, Lady Ethelde. I assumed my parents or Sir Ennoh would've told you."

He straightened, filling out the folds of his dark gray cloak with his broad frame. "If they'd told me, wouldn't they have instructed me to accompany you?"

I swallowed against the sudden dryness in my throat. "Not in this case, since I'm first meeting up with a party of friends for a picnic. Twenty, in fact, which is why we brought so many supplies." I patted the bulging pack strapped in front of Tassie's blanket.

A giggle nearly bubbled up, despite the dire situation. If pressed, I doubted I could name twenty friends who lived near enough to join me for an afternoon. But it was the same story I'd asked Nadette to pass on to the kitchen staff, as I wouldn't need half so much food for a quick jaunt up to Lady Ethelde's manor.

His lips twisted at one corner in an expression that would've almost been endearing if not for the suspicion in his eyes. "A picnic for twenty." He looked around, as though expecting more dining companions to materialize from the tall grasses swaying around us.

"We haven't met up with them yet, as you can see." I forced my fingers not to fiddle with Tassie's reins. "But I brought along Nadette, so there's nothing untoward about our outing and you needn't—"

"Just how far away is this picnic, exactly?" The impudent man never hesitated to interrupt me. As though being a few years older somehow gave him vastly superior authority and wisdom.

"Beyond the castle gates." The answer was true enough, if a bit vague.

His brows rose. "You're already well beyond the castle gates. Why did you not ask me to escort you?"

Because once you discovered there wasn't a picnic, you'd march me right back home again. "There was no need to trouble you. I shall be perfectly safe once surrounded by my companions."

"All nineteen of them, yes." He scratched at a scruffy spot on his jawline he'd apparently neglected to shave. "If you would, Princess, humor me and allow me to see you safely to your friends."

I raised my chin. "Surely the king has something more important for you to accomplish than to ride around the countryside with Nadette and I all afternoon."

"My primary duty is your safety, Your Highness. As you well know." Hurt and chagrin flickered in his eyes before they darkened with mistrust once more.

I winced. Hopefully only internally. From the moment he'd been assigned as my personal guard nearly a year before, he'd made it clear he was less than thrilled with the task. "Of course, my apologies. You are diligent in your work, and I'm grateful for the offer. But I have no wish to inconvenience you for such a trifling outing. To bore you, really, since we'll likely chat long into the afternoon. I'm well aware that idleness is difficult for a knight to bear, and you'll think our games frivolous after all your training and discipline..."

Nadette cleared her throat.

Sir Albrecht tilted his head. "You're not actually meeting friends for a picnic at all, are you?"

"What?" I willed my eyes to not flare in panic. Tassie gave a short squeak and shifted beneath me. I dug my fingers into her warm, coarse fur. "I most certainly am. Why else would I request so much food? You know, it's insulting to a young lady to insinuate that she might plan to eat—"

"You always babble when you're lying." Sir Albrecht tightened his grip on his reins.

"Lying?" I tossed my head, which was disappointingly unsatisfactory since my hair was coiled into a chignon at the base of my neck. "When have I lied to you?"

"When you hid a bird in your chambers, when you tried to sneak off for a nighttime ride, when you forgot the dinner with that foreign diplomat..."

My foot itched to stomp, but I didn't want to hurt Tassie or unbalance myself. "I didn't forget, I was merely late. If you had any appreciation of nature, you would've understood the nighttime ride. And I was trying to nurse the bird back to good health. In every case, I had a very reasonable explanation."

He sighed. "And what is your reasonable explanation this time, Princess?"

I pressed a hand to my forehead. *What now?* I could hardly prove my non-existent picnic wasn't a falsehood. And Sir Albrecht apparently had no intention of turning back to the castle without a better excuse.

Swallowing a grunt, I faced him. "You're right, there's no picnic. Would you believe that I don't like the food served at Lady Ethelde's manor and decided to bring some of my own?"

His responding sigh might've carried a hint of a laugh.

"Fine." I leaned more heavily against Tassie for support. "I'm not going to Lady Ethelde's. I needed an excuse to leave the castle for a few weeks in order to find someone who I believe can solve the dilemma between my sister and Pappa. You may return to Telynn Castle and recruit a search party to drag me back home, but by then I'll be hiding on the mountainside. So the more straightforward option would be to"—*ugh, how had it come to this?*— "accompany us."

Anger had replaced the amusement in his expression. "You planned to set off on a multi-week journey without any guards? Without telling your family where you're going?" He directed his gaze to the heavens, as though expecting the Holy One to commiserate with him. "How were you planning to survive? How will you stay safe?"

"As I already explained, we brought plenty of food. Plus bedrolls, quilts, and warm clothes." I patted one of the packs dangling in front of my knees. "A few nights outdoors won't hurt—"

"But what of wild animals? Of brigands who would salivate at the sight of two well-dressed women traveling alone?"

With a tug, I straightened the buttoned burgundy vest I'd worn over a long-sleeved tan dress of soft cotton. Clothing Nadette had scrounged for me from the servants' spare supplies. "I'm dressed far more simply than my usual attire." I patted the pocket hidden in the layers of my split skirt. "And I never travel without a dagger. Sir Ennoh has taught me to wield it."

"A dagger." He shook his head, teeth gritted. "You were just telling me there have been problems with Markou. Your disappearance will no doubt worsen the conflict, if not incite a war."

I brushed his concerns away along with a fluffy white seed floating in the breeze. "Prince Carre has his sights set on Verena. No one in Markou will care if I go gallivanting around the countryside. And I'm hardly disappearing when I've announced a visit to Lady Ethelde."

"But if you don't return?"

I huffed. "I have every intention of returning."

"Of course you do." Wincing, he turned his stormy glare on my lady's maid. "Lady Nadette, how could you possibly condone this? You know the king and queen would never approve."

Poor Nadette toyed with her reins, her knuckles white. "Her Highness feels the quest is of the utmost importance. I knew she'd find a way to leave the castle one way or another, so at least now she's not alone."

The hard set of his jaw softened a fraction. "Your loyalty does you credit. And no doubt you're right that your foolhardy charge would've left entirely on her own if she felt it was the only way." He ran a hand through his hair, his posture tense. "I suppose that leaves me no choice but to accompany you, unless you'll give me a chance to talk you out of this ill-advised scheme."

I tried to make my gaze as stern as his. "I'm going with or without you."

He gestured forward. "Then let's be off, before I can think better of it."

Irritation nipped at my insides. In moments, I'd gone from rejoicing at my freedom to being scolded and tied down by this grump of a knight. "You realize our food supplies won't be enough if they have to be shared between three people instead of two." *Please, decide not to come. And not to tell my parents and cause them to be furious with me...*

He waved my concern aside. "I can supplement them with game as necessary. Hunting and trapping won't be a problem, possibly even fishing, depending on our location." He furrowed his brow. "Just what is our planned destination?"

"The Province of Ormande." I faced forward, avoiding his gaze.

"Ormande?" Incredulity laced his tone. "But—"

"Northward, we go!" Sweeping my hand toward the Norden Mountains, I pressed my heel against Tassie's side. *Quick, girl. If you gallop off fast enough, perhaps we can avoid another lecture.*

"How was your first night sleeping out of doors, Princess?" Sir Albrecht rode up beside me as we slowed our elk to a walk for a rocky stretch of path. The smirk on his face indicated he anticipated a negative answer.

We'd camped beneath soft moonlight in the lower hills of the Norden Mountains. The stars had shown more brightly than ever, and the weather was fair, aside from the hint of winter's chill still lingering after the sun disappeared below the horizon. The campfire's glow had been cozy, and despite Sir Albrecht's presence, I'd been in a cheerful mood.

He hadn't put a stop to my quest, after all.

But once we'd each settled beneath our quilts for the night, my optimism had taken a dip. As it turned out, the ground was cold, hard, and wet—hardly a fit place for sleeping.

I wasn't about to admit that to him, though, so I pasted on a bright smile. "Delightful. Surrounded by fresh air, beautiful stars, and the peaceful sounds only nature can provide. I can't imagine anything better."

"Hmm." He studied me, one brow raised in a sardonic tilt. "Well, then, it's fortunate for you we have so many more nights under the stars ahead of us. Are you ready to tell me what's taking us to Ormande? I'm too far along on this journey now to turn back and alert your parents, and you can't keep me in the dark forever."

He had a valid point. I slid my thumb and forefinger along the leather of Tassie's reins. "Do you remember Sir Jonas? He was a knight at Telynn Castle, perhaps six or seven years ago?"

"I would've been a squire at that time, still in training." He tilted his head. "Was he the clumsy one who was always dropping his sword?"

I suppressed a grin. *Poor Sir Jonas.* "Yes, that was likely him. He was Verena's assigned guard for a time before he was sent to serve Lord Hamelun in Ormande."

"He was sent all the way up there?" Sir Albrecht's eyes widened before narrowing in confusion. "But why would you need to contact him now? On a trek unsanctioned by the king and queen? You said this had something to do with your sister's suitors..." His breath caught on a quick inhale. "Were he and your sister—?"

I swatted his arm. "Nothing inappropriate, no. Don't go starting any rumors."

He snorted. "Do I strike you as a source of information for local gossips?"

"I know very little about how you interact with others at the castle. Or if you deign to talk with anyone at all." I scrunched my nose at him. "But as for Sir Jonas, my sister was quite fond of him. I recall him making her laugh more than anyone I've ever seen." Or, at least, Verena seemed to have such recollections.

"He must've been in love with Princess Verena, then, if you think he'll be willing to travel back to Telynn Castle."

I nibbled at my lip. "He never declared himself to Verena. But they seemed to develop quite a bond of friendship while he was assigned to her."

"Friendship?" His voice took on a harsher tone. "And you think when you explain the situation, this man will just follow you like a puppy to potentially marry a woman he hasn't seen—probably hasn't thought about—in seven years? Princess, you can't honestly expect—"

"Perhaps not expect, but I do hope." I forced my growing anxiety out with a puff of air. Time to distract the pessimistic Sir Albrecht from this line of conversation. "Do you think it's wise to refer to me as Princess while we're out in the wild?"

He shook his head. "What?"

"Yesterday, you were so concerned about bandits and whatnot. Wouldn't it draw their attention if they were to hear you call me Princess? Might it not be wiser to use just my name for the duration of our journey?"

"I hadn't given it any thought." He flicked away a burr that had stuck to his mount's neck. "I doubt it will be a concern as long as I can restrain myself from shouting at you over the next week or two."

If not riding on the back of an elk, I would've planted my fists on my hips. "Given our unpromising start, that doesn't seem very likely, does it? Please, call me Liesel."

He glanced back to where my lady's maid followed closely behind. "I'm not sure Lady Nadette, or your parents, for that matter, would condone such familiarity."

"Nor would they condone me sleeping on the ground beside a campfire, so it's hardly relevant." I gave a playful shrug. *So far, so good, with the distraction.* "And while we're on the subject of names, Sir Albrecht is really quite a mouthful."

His brows furrowed. "You have an objection to my name?"

I gestured vaguely with my free hand. "No objection, per se, it's just long. May I at least leave off the Sir?"

His chest rose and fell as though suppressing a sigh. "If you must."

"Albrecht, hmm." My lips puckered to the side. "It's still a bit cumbersome."

"No longer than Liesel, Your Highness." His tone had lowered with poorly-subdued irritation.

"I suppose, yet it feels longer." I turned to Nadette, who walked Hilde up beside Tassie. "Wouldn't you agree?"

Her wide eyes shifted between me and my guard. "Sir Albrecht is a fine name, milady."

"Why, thank you." His self-satisfied smile made me bristle.

I should've known sweet Nadette would opt for an uncontroversial opinion. Tapping my chin, I gave an exaggerated hum. "I think I'll call you Breck. If you don't object." *Probably even if you do.*

He choked on a surprised cough. "Breck?"

"Yes, it suits you." I extended my hand. "Very, you know, dashing."

His jaw twitched. "If you insist, Princess."

"Excellent. I'm glad we have that settled. Though if I'm going to call you something as informal as Breck, you really must call me Liesel."

"I'm beginning to think I should've just believed you about that picnic." He rubbed his forehead.

I flicked Tassie's reins. "Now you've learned your lesson for next time. I believe Nadette has some of her herbs packed if you're suffering from a headache."

"I do, indeed." Nadette nodded eagerly.

Breck coughed. "A lot of them, I hope."

I grinned. "Enough for twenty picnickers, of course."

His wince couldn't entirely hide his twitch of a smile. "Of course."

Chapter 5

"PRINCESS?"

I blinked as something jostled my shoulder.

"Princess Liesel? Wake up."

"What…" Suppressing a shiver, I squinted at the frowning man stooped over me. Cold from the hard ground had seeped into my very bones. A second night sleeping outdoors hadn't improved the experience. "Breck? What's wrong?"

"Where is your supply pack?" His eyes held a frantic glint I'd never seen.

"My—" Rubbing my icy hands together, I sat up. "Right here, acting as a most uncomfortable pillow."

He released a long exhale. "Does it seem to be intact?"

"I think so." Craning my stiff neck from side to side, I pulled the pack onto my lap and inspected it. "Looks fine to me. Why?"

"Thank the snows we still have some of our provisions, then." He pointed to the far end of the clearing and shook his head. "The packs Lady Nadette and I have been carrying didn't fare so well."

"They didn't? But..." My groggy mind struggled to make sense of his words as I sat up and pulled on my half boots. I followed him past where he'd slept on the other side of the fire and into the trees. He paused at a particularly wide trunk with reddish bark.

I directed my gaze upward, and a gasp clawed at my throat. The packs he'd so carefully strung high in the branches were slashed, our food stores reduced to crumbs scattered in the grass below.

"Oh no." I searched the surrounding trees, as though their whispering needles could give an explanation. "What creature could reach so high?"

"I've been wondering the same thing. And why didn't they go after the far more accessible pack lying foolishly on the ground?" He directed a glare my way before kneeling beside the mess that used to be our carefully-packed food.

I ran the ruined fabric through my fingers. The tear was rough, but... I glanced toward the clearing where Nadette still slept near the fire's dying embers and kept my voice low. "Was it an animal at all? Or was this the work of a knife?"

"Another question I've asked myself." He searched the ground, brows drawn. "This trampled underbrush makes it impossible to tell if there are footprints."

"Wouldn't the presence of a person—or that large of an animal—alarm the elk?"

He pressed his lips into a thin line. "Perhaps not, from the other side of the clearing. Especially if they were asleep. We've been running them hard the past few days."

I nodded. Tassie and the others had been munching on grass where we'd tethered them to the trees, seemingly undisturbed.

"What now?" I lifted a pack from the tree, my stomach sinking at its lack of weight. The remains of biscuits, dried fruit and meat, potatoes, and cheese littered the ground—now a feast for birds and squirrels. "These contained over half our food stores, and we aren't even—" I caught myself before my voice could squeak higher. *Stop it, Liesel. No one wants to deal with your hysteria.*

"I take full responsibility, Your Highness." Breck ducked his head. "I should've been more vigilant. To think something—possibly some-one—got near enough to do you harm, and I wasn't on alert to defend you…"

Swallowing my panic, I forced a gentle tone. "No, Breck. You need sleep, too. It demonstrates wisdom that you kept the supplies at a distance from us so we didn't share their fate."

He shifted his feet, keeping his gaze downcast.

Time to lighten the mood. I heaved a dramatic sigh. "Well, so much for our picnic."

Breck glanced up. His smile was wry, but it erased the line between his brows. "No doubt your twenty guests will be disappointed."

"Indeed." I gathered the other pack, searching for what we could salvage. "But this way, you'll get to show off your hunting prowess."

He grimaced. "I'd hoped not to waste that much time."

"Perhaps you might teach me? Then we could hunt together and get twice the game." I blinked up at him with wide, innocent eyes.

"I can handle it." He gave an elaborate shudder. "Just imagine what mischief you might get into with a bow in your hands."

"If you insist." I shrugged and headed back to the clearing to see if my pack could hold any of our salvageable supplies.

"But Princess." Breck halted my progress with a hand on my wrist. "Take every caution. Whatever—or whoever—tampered with our supplies may not have gone far."

Restlessness plagued me as I crunched on a hard biscuit and gathered my few possessions to place back into Tassie's packs. Breck claimed we'd covered more than half the distance to Ormande, and we'd only been traveling for three days.

Excitement, not weariness, should be thrumming through my veins.

But I hadn't gotten a good night of sleep in nearly a week, between my plans for departure and the unrelenting cold, hard dirt we camped on each night. The forested mountainside, bursting with the vibrant blossoms and birdsong of spring, felt a bit foreboding with the mystery of our ravaged supplies haunting us like a specter.

Our reduced food stores would barely last until we reached Sir Jonas, unless we slowed to allow Breck to do more hunting. I recoiled at the memory of the poor rabbit he'd roasted the night before.

We'd have to pray that Lord Hamelun would be generous enough to send some provisions along for our return journey.

Pray. My hands stilled. It was Siebennet. A glance at the sun confirmed my family would likely be attending a service at the chapel this very moment, commemorating the death and resurrection of the Holy One's Son. I envisioned the gilt-edged engravings on our reserved pew, Father Lars's gentle admonitions, Mamma's lovely singing, the deep conviction in Pappa's voice as he recited prayers. *Do they miss me? Have they any suspicions that I'm not traveling anywhere near Lady Ethelde's manor?*

My shoulders sagged as I looked toward Nadette, who was feeding the elk crinkled apples she'd found strewn beneath the trees. I'd taken her away from her friends, family, and weekly worship as well.

"Nadette." I glanced in the direction of the stream, where Breck had disappeared to wash. Hopefully he wouldn't return for a time yet. "I just realized we're missing the Siebennet service. It feels a bit...odd, doesn't it?"

She nodded with a sad smile. "Indeed it does, milady. But if the weather holds and Sir Jonas is cooperative, we ought to be back in our usual seats at the chapel next week."

My heart lifted a bit. "That is a cheering thought. For today, do you think we should..." I scratched at the thick collar of my dress. "Would you like to pray with me?"

Relinquishing her last apple, she turned fully toward me. "What a lovely idea, Princess Liesel. I'd like that very much."

I nodded, encouraged but still plagued by awkwardness. Despite attending services every Siebennet and other holidays, my faith had always been very private. Thoughts directed at the Holy One, prayers whispered at my bedside.

Never anything spoken aloud in front of my family, even, let alone servants.

"Perhaps we could... There." I gestured to a low, wide stone. "Would it work to kneel here, do you think?"

"Let's give it a try." Nadette scurried to the rock and dropped to her knees, as though her role included testing out potentially uncomfortable kneelers before they injured my royal legs. "Yes, I think it will do nicely. As long as we aren't in this position too long, at any rate."

With a laugh, I knelt at her side. The sweet woman was trying so hard to accommodate my odd request.

I folded my hands and bowed my head. *Now what? Perhaps I should've...*

"Would you like me to begin, milady?" Nadette nudged my arm.

"Yes, please." Relief huffed out on my breathy tone.

She closed her eyes, and I followed suit.

"Holy One, we are so thankful for the beauty of your creation. We thank you for keeping us safe thus far on our journey. Please help us to be ever mindful of You, especially on this day that we set apart for Your praise." Pausing, she glanced to me. "Would you like to add something, milady?"

"Oh, yes." I pressed my eyelids shut once more. "Holy One, I am thankful for the companionship of Nadette on this quest. For—"

"Princess? Lady Nadette?" Breck's voice rang out in panic.

Couldn't he have waited a few more minutes? Cheeks heating, I rose. "We're over here, Breck. Everything's fine."

He jogged closer, shaking moisture from his damp hair. He looked a bit more unruly, less burdened, somehow, with his hair in soggy disarray and uneven scruff shading his jaw. I suppressed a wince. The poor man hadn't had an opportunity to even bring an extra set of clothes, let alone a way to shave more cleanly than with a knife.

His gaze hastily took us in. "You're unhurt? Why were you—?"

"Princess Liesel thought we ought to say a brief prayer in honor of Siebennet." Nadette jumped in, clearly eager to avoid an argument. "Gracious, how we must've startled you."

His brows rose. "No need to apologize. I'm glad all is well."

Nadette resumed her kneeling position, then gestured toward Breck. "Would you care to join us?"

The warmth searing my face spread down my neck. Of course she felt she had to ask, but...

"I would. Thank you." *What?* No discernible irony or disdain crossed his features. He gestured to let me kneel first, then lowered himself at my side.

Nadette tilted her head toward me. "Princess Liesel was just taking her turn in prayer."

No, no, no. But there was no way out of it now. Clenching my teeth, I folded my hands. *Help me to make this about You, Holy One. Not about the irritating guard at my side who smells like pine trees and fresh soap...*

I cleared my throat. "Holy One, I thank you for providing companions on my quest. Thank you for this opportunity to aid in Verena's happiness. Please guide our steps as we journey onward. Help us to...to fulfill our goal and return to Telynn Castle in safety. Look after my family while we're gone, and bless us. And Sir Jonas. Help us to find him, and give him the courage to join us." *And comfort me in my disappointment if he refuses.* "Amen." My folded hands trembled as the doubt that weighed upon my heart seeped into my consciousness.

Nadette patted my arm. "Would you like to add anything, Sir Albrecht?"

I kept my eyes squeezed shut, hearing him shift beside me.

"Bring healing to my father, Holy One, if it is Your will. Don't let his condition worsen while I'm away. Comfort our family, and help us to cherish whatever time we have left with him. Fill us with the hope that we will one day be reunited in paradise with You for all eternity. Amen."

Nadette closed our little makeshift service with a few recited prayers. I mumbled the words, my mind straying to the quiet man beside me.

His father was dying? While I'd dragged him across the countryside?

We rose, and I brushed off my skirt. Today's ensemble was a muted gray-blue. How I missed the vibrant colors of my gowns back home. But these simple dresses were comfortable, and more importantly, far less likely to draw attention.

Breck stepped away from the rock. "Will you be ready to depart soon, Princess?" Did emotion deepen his tone, or had I imagined it?

I tried to convey sympathy with a gentle smile. "Yes, I just need to strap my packs on Tassie."

He shook his head. "Allow me." Before I could respond, he strode across the clearing to the elk.

After stooping to gather my things, I followed.

I stood self-consciously to the side as he tightened the straps of Tassie's blanket around her midsection. "Breck?"

"Mmm?" His focus remained on his task.

"I—I'm sorry."

His practiced movements hesitated. Straightening, he turned to me with furrowed brows. "Sorry for what?"

"For taking you away from your family when your father is ailing." I shifted the material draped awkwardly across my arm. "I'm sure it's difficult, not knowing how he fares. I had no idea…"

"I know." He took the quilt and bedroll from me and turned back to Tassie. "And if you recall, you adamantly did *not* want me to accompany you on this journey. So it would hardly be fair for me to place the blame on you."

"I suppose, but still…" The lump in my chest seemed to grow heavier with every word, but I had to continue. "You were just trying to fulfill your duties. You certainly never would've been halfway through the Norden Mountains to Ormande if it weren't for my recklessness."

With a final tug on the rope securing my bedding, he met my gaze. "My father is ailing, yes. It's always hard to be away from him. But the progression of the illness has been slow in recent months. I doubt there will be any noticeable change by the time I return." He lifted the pack dangling from my wrist. "My place is to serve the royal family, wherever I'm needed. My family and I knew that when I presented myself to be trained as a knight."

"Still, I apologize for being the cause of your prolonged separation from your family." I twined my now-empty arms around my midsection. "I hope your father is able to recover, or that he at least isn't in too much pain."

His lips pressed into what could almost pass as a smile. "Thank you, Princess." He patted Tassie's neck. "She should be all ready to go. Let me untie Klaus, and we can be on our way."

"Breck." I clutched his sleeve before he could attend to his elk.

His eyes widened a fraction, regarding my hand on his arm before returning to my face.

I swallowed, my throat inexplicably dry. "I also wanted to say...thank you. Despite my initial attempts to turn you away, I'm very grateful that you joined us on what I'm sure you consider to be a fool's errand. I know you'd rather be anywhere else, but you've been most helpful and I feel much safer with you accompanying us."

"I'm glad." His gaze warmed before taking on a teasing glint. "And fool's errand this may be, but I wouldn't miss the chance to hear you convince this Sir Jonas to come home with you and devise a plan to make your dour sister laugh. And if successful, marry her and one day become king."

I massaged my forehead. *When he put it like that...*

"Don't let me dampen your bright hopes, Princess." He grazed his thumb across the back of my hand in a surprisingly tender gesture. "If anyone can convince him, it's you."

Chapter 6

"Do you think I can convince Cook to make some lemon tarts when we get home? Or raspberry strudel? Or maybe cinnamon buns..." My mouth watered at the thought of warm baked goods, especially after a morning rain shower had left us cold and soggy. How I longed to eat something other than roasted, unseasoned meat, stale biscuits, and berries.

Nadette inhaled sharply. "Gracious, milady! What a stomachache you'd suffer from all those treats. Better to ask her to make you one variety at a time."

"I'd share with you, of course." Count on Nadette to be intimidated even by the prospect of too many desserts. "But you're probably right. It might be suspicious if I were to return to the castle acting like I hadn't eaten a decent meal in—"

Ahead, Breck grunted and pulled his elk, Klaus, to a halt. "I was afraid it might come to this."

Pushing thoughts of pastries aside, I nudged Tassie to speed up until we reached him. "Might come to what?"

He extended his hand to indicate a rock face with broad tan streaks etched across the gray.

"I think it's quite pretty." The stone curved into almost a scalloped shape, forming little semi-circular ledges at irregular intervals.

He huffed. "Pretty it may be, but it's in our way."

"Surely we can…" My words died out as I took in the problem. The rock wall rose in every direction that would allow us to make forward progress.

Nadette joined us, her green eyes wide. "Oh, my. Should we turn around? I believe we passed a fork in the path a while back."

A long while back. I cringed at the prospect of so much time lost.

Breck shook his head. "No, this is the shortest way." He patted Klaus's neck. "I'm afraid we'll have to complete the final leg of our journey on foot."

"On foot? Surely not." I sank against Tassie. "What about the elk?"

Breck's smile was tight, but likely meant to be reassuring. "This is the fastest route by far. And the elk will be all right for a few days on their own." With a final glare at the rock face, he turned Klaus around. "Let's find them a shady clearing with some grass to munch on and water within reach. We'll tie them securely but with plenty of length so they won't feel too confined."

Swallowing a wave of emotion, I nodded. "All right. If it's the only way."

He paused at my side to give my arm a quick pat. "They'll be fine. I wouldn't be surprised if they're grateful for the break."

"True." I glanced back at the uneven rock ledges. Figuring out a way to climb up was likely to be a fun adventure.

Nadette stroked Hilde's taupe neck. "You poor dears. We'll pray for the Holy One's protection over you while we're gone."

Once Breck had pulled Klaus ahead, I looped my arms around Tassie. "You'll just need to hang tight for a few days, dear girl. I'll be back for you as soon as I can."

My heels kicked the rock I sat on in a rhythmic cadence. *Click, click, click.* After walking for a full day, I appreciated and missed my elk more than ever.

We'll reach Sir Jonas tomorrow. I'd kept the refrain echoing through my mind all morning, up a steep rocky path and now through this narrow channel.

A tall shadow loomed over me. "How goes your attempt at resting your legs?"

I squinted up at Breck. "Better than yours. At least I'm sitting."

He huffed a chuckle. "I'm keeping an eye on our surroundings."

"Then I'll join you." I pushed myself to standing and stretched my neck. "I'm anxious to be on our way again."

"You don't say?" His brows rose in mock query.

I paced away from him. "I can't help it. It makes me uneasy to be separated from Tassie. And we're so close. I just want to put this leg of our journey behind us. These high cliffs make me feel boxed in."

"I can hardly fault you for that." He tugged at the lacing pulling his collar tight. In the sun's growing warmth, he'd removed his cloak and draped it over his arm.

"Yet I'm sure you do, anyway." I scrunched my nose at him before turning toward the little dip in the wall where Nadette had disappeared to freshen up. "But poor Nadette deserves a break. The dear woman never complains, but I think the walk has made her even more nervous than usual."

He leaned his hand against the rough rock face. "She'll make it through. Despite her fretting, she's tougher than I would've expected. Once we arrive at Lord Hamelun's tomorrow, we'll get a decent meal or two and a night in a real bed. It should do us all good."

"Yes, I am looking forward to that." I kicked a pebble down the path. "If I'd known we'd have to travel on foot for so long, perhaps I shouldn't have—"

"Liesel." My name sounded like a command as he shoved me against the cliff, beneath a small outcropping. Above, an odd scraping sound grew increasingly louder.

I pounded against his chest. "Ouch. Unhand me! What..." My protest died in a squeak as a giant boulder landed where I'd just been standing.

"Are you all right?" Breck peered into my face as he pushed even closer.

"I—I think so. But what's happening?" The sound of skittering rocks echoed in every direction.

He glanced over his shoulder. "Some kind of avalanche."

"An avalanche? In fine weather in the spring?" Confusion further muddled my panic-stricken mind.

"Or a landslide? It doesn't make sense to me, either. I haven't seen evidence of other travelers, but perhaps..." His gaze locked with mine once more, and his words trailed off.

Our faces were mere inches apart, his breadth pressing me tightly against the stone cliff. This close, gold flecks appeared in his amber eyes. I'd always grudgingly acknowledged Breck was handsome, but I'd never before been so *aware* of him.

Thank the snows he wasn't called upon to save my life often.

Dryness coated my throat as the moment stretched on. *Look away, Liesel.* But somehow, I couldn't.

More stones clattered above.

Breck tipped his head even closer. "Shut your eyes." His urgent whisper blew warm air across my forehead.

Behind us, stones pelted the ground like a hailstorm.

I squeezed my eyes shut, my fingers clenching the coarse fabric of his tunic.

Breck shifted one arm to curve around my back, keeping the other braced on the stone. "I won't let anything hurt you."

"I know." I felt the truth of the statement deep in my core. For all our bickering, Breck wouldn't hesitate to sacrifice himself if it meant keeping me safe. *Please, Holy One, don't let it come to that.* I dipped my head until it rested on his shoulder.

Our tense embrace likely only lasted for a handful of minutes, but it felt like an eternity as the mountain seemed to crumble around us. After the silence gave way to renewed birdsong, Breck's grip on my back released.

"Is it over?" I cringed at my childish tone.

"I think so. But stay here a moment." He patted my hair as though I were a well-behaved puppy.

I took more comfort from the awkward gesture than I should've.

Edging away, he turned to survey the damage. I rose up on my toes and peeked over his shoulder. Rocks of varying sizes filled the gap between cliff faces almost to my shoulder level, making the path impassable.

"Nadette." Her name escaped my lips in a whimper.

Breck squeezed my shoulder. "This seems pretty localized. If she was still by the stream, she should be unharmed."

My breath eased out in a hiss. "I hope so."

"Unfortunately, it might be hours before we know for sure. This won't be easy to clear." With a poorly-suppressed growl, he hefted the nearest rock and lobbed it farther down the path.

I stepped to his side, giving the rising peak a wary glance. All seemed quiet, undisturbed. If not for the dust floating in the air and the pile of rocks before us, one would think it a dull afternoon. Tugging my tapered sleeves to my elbows, I reached for my first stone.

"Princess, no." Breck paused to shake his head. "This is hardly a task suitable for a lady. I can't ask you to clear rubble like a common laborer."

"You're not asking." My next rock landed with a *thunk* beside the path. "And neither am I. I have no intention of uselessly lounging here in the shade while you do all the work. I want to see Nadette, I want to get out of this mountain pass, and I want to return to Tassie. All of that requires clearing this path, so let's get it done."

His breath released in a half-huff, half-chuckle. "If you insist, Princess, I won't be the one to stop you." He hefted another rock, then glanced back at me. "I must say, Nadette isn't the only one who's tougher than I expected."

"Princess? Princess!" The distant call grew louder, twining its way into my hazy brain.

I squinted at the rock in my arms. *Who could...Nadette!* I flung the stone with renewed energy, my arms nearly limp after what felt like hours of lifting. "We're here, Nadette!"

"Milady?" The word ended in a choked sob as Nadette's face appeared on the other side of the now knee-high rock pile.

"Oh, Nadette, you're all right." Tears crowded my eyes as I surged forward, ignoring Breck's protests. I slipped and stumbled over the unsteady heap of stones until I staggered across to Nadette's side.

She enveloped me in a tight hug. "Milady, you're alive. I thought for certain..." She squeezed me tighter, then leaned back to study me. "Are you truly unharmed?"

I attempted a grin that probably landed closer to a grimace. "Frightened to distraction and hoping to never see another rock again in my life, but I'm well. Thank the Holy One for Breck's quick reaction—he pushed me out of the way before I even noticed the landslide. He likely saved my life."

I glanced back to where Breck had paused in his stone removal to swipe a hand across his brow.

Even from this distance, his warm gaze held a hint of the charged energy I'd felt under the ledge.

"I'm grateful no one was hurt." His eyes held mine for another moment before shifting to Nadette. "We hoped you were far enough from the path to be unharmed."

"Yes, yes, I was still by the creek. What a ninny I was, taking so much time to wash when we could've been on our way and past the danger if I'd hurried." She shook her head. "What a ruckus it made! Seemed to shake the very mountainside. I confess I hid for some time, not knowing what could be the cause or whether it might start up again."

Breck nodded as he hefted a stone half the size of a barrel. "That was wise."

I patted Nadette's hand. "And of course you couldn't have predicted such a catastrophe. I'm glad your stop at the stream kept you safe."

"Well, once I finally summoned some nerve, I left my hiding place. I'd been worried enough, then to see the path in such a state. In the very place you'd been standing. Good gracious!" She flapped her hand before her face like a frantic fan. "I'd been worried about you before, but that sent me into a right state. I charged up and down that rise, looking for a place to cross. It's clear not too far ahead and behind us not three elk-lengths. But imagine what I thought when I didn't find you on either end." Her nose scrunched as she let out an anguished little wail.

"What a fright you've had. To be alone all that time, not knowing what had become of us." I smoothed her sleeves from shoulder to elbow. "But we are well, as you can see, and I'm grateful to hear there are less of these miserable rocks to move than I originally thought."

Breck grunted his agreement as he sent an armful of smaller stones clattering down the path.

I gave Nadette's hands one last squeeze before turning to rejoin him. "Is it typical for landslides to be so localized?"

Breck's brows lowered. "I suspect nothing about this rockslide could be considered typical."

I paused, glancing up from my crouch. "You don't think it was natural?"

"I don't see how it's possible." He shook his head, jostling loose, sweat-dampened hair onto his forehead. "None of it makes sense unless someone saw us on the path and sent those rocks to hinder us, at the least, or else..."

"Or else to crush us." Despite my exertion, a shiver coursed down my back. "But why? Are people in these mountains so desperate for isolation that they'd injure innocent travelers who happen to venture too near?"

Nadette gave a little sniff of alarm, her head pivoting between the two of us.

"Perhaps." Breck pressed his lips together, then turned away to lift another stone.

I recognized that look. "But that's not your theory. You think someone wanted to hurt us specifically?"

He shrugged, avoiding my gaze.

My chest sank under the weight of an internal avalanche. "You think they're trying to hurt *me*."

"It makes the most sense." His eyes radiated sympathy and determination. "But I have no intention of letting them."

"Nor I." Nadette tried to set her jaw, her chin quivering. "But oh, milady, you must be careful."

"Of course I will." I gave her hand a squeeze. "But aside from you two insisting on using my formal title, how would they even know it's me?" I clutched my tan cotton skirt in a desperate protest. "I'm dressed like a commoner, and I didn't travel with a large retinue of servants and guards."

"True." A hint of irony lightened Breck's expression. "But they might've followed us from Telynn Castle. And thanks to your mother's Joran descent, you and your sister have darker hair than almost anyone else in Walthar. It makes you look...distinctive."

Desperate to disperse my rising fears, I batted my lashes at him in mock flirtation. "Distinctive in a good way?"

He snorted. "Distinctive in a dangerous way."

Chapter 7

"WHO GOES THERE?" THE harsh call shattered the peaceful rhythm of our footsteps interspersed with the chattering of the small, reddish squirrels that seemed to inhabit every nearby tree. My steps faltered as I struggled to keep my expression neutral.

We'd made it to Ormande. After picking our way through the remaining rubble of that dreadful pass, we'd trudged up another steep incline before the path descended to a sparkling lake. We skirted around the lake's edge, the glorious view only impeded by a brown bear Breck had to frighten off when it seemed to catch the scent of the remaining scraps of food in our packs. Now he estimated we'd reach Lord Hamelun's vast estate within the hour.

We can't be intercepted when we're so close.

Breck strode to the front of our little party. "We come in peace." His voice didn't quaver, but his shoulders had lost their relaxed slant.

Nadette sidled up beside me. "Oh, milady, you'd best get out your dagger. You don't think this is the man who..." Judging by her tense stance and wide eyes, she seemed torn between retreating and throwing herself in front of me.

Her unfinished whisper echoed my own fearful questions. Could this be the mysterious stranger who had caused the landslide? Who seemed intent on killing me? The man who lumbered into view carried a spear, but his blue and gold tunic appeared to be a uniform of some sort.

I swallowed, heaving deep breaths to calm my racing pulse. "It's not likely that after all the secrecy he would now present himself to us in such a forward manner. Especially when he's outnumbered." The uniform's significance brought a genuine smile. "Perhaps we've finally reached Lord Hamelun's land."

Nadette stayed close, but the corners of her mouth twitched. "Gracious, I do hope you're right."

The man reached us, brows raised. "Not many venture this far north, unless they're with a larger company. What is your business here?"

Breck inclined his head but kept a hand resting on his sword hilt. "I can understand why—the journey is not for the faint of spirit. We've come to request a favor of Lord Hamelun. Is his fortress nearby?"

"It is, indeed." He narrowed his gaze. "But what is your connection to him? Tell me the nature of this favor."

Breck's shoulders rose and fell the way they did when he was restraining an exasperated sigh. "Your protectiveness does you credit, sir. But I can assure you, we mean your master no harm."

I straightened my spine and angled my jaw to a slightly haughty stance. Covered in leaves and dirt or not, I was still a princess. "The favor concerns the Waltharian royal family. I'm here to make the request myself." I brushed off my skirt, then stepped out from behind Breck. Extending my left hand, I displayed the signet ring circling my third finger.

Confusion pinched the broad guard's features as he drew near enough to squint at the ring. "Royal family? But..." Eyes widening, he hurriedly ducked into a bow. "You're one of the princesses, then? Forgive me, but I never would've expected...that is, we weren't given word—"

"There is nothing to forgive. Please rise." No need to make the poor man babble in his embarrassment. "I am Princess Liesel, this is my guard, Sir Albrecht, and my maid, Lady Nadette. We have had a long journey and would appreciate if you could escort us to the fortress at once."

"Of course, Your Highness. My apologies for the delay." Darting us another uncertain glance, he gestured behind him. "Please, follow me."

Breck caught my eye as we shuffled forward, his expression something between impressed and amused. He held out his arm with a bow. "I suppose I'd best show the proper respect, *Your Highness.*"

With an imperious flick of my filthy hair, I looped my fingers around his elbow. "If you must, but don't slow me down." Beyond this rise, shelter and food awaited. Hopefully even a warm bath.

"You're sure it's *me* she asked for?"

I sat up at the low, muffled question so near the parlor door. The comfort of warm food in my stomach, the knots brushed from my hair, and a clean dress had nearly lulled me to sleep.

"Do you know of another Sir Jonas on the estate?" The second voice was clipped with impatience. "Don't keep the princess waiting, man."

The door eased open, and I rose. After an opportunity to wash and eat, a servant had escorted me to this comfortable but unadorned parlor to meet with Sir Jonas. Lord Hamelun had already given his permission for the knight to return to the castle with us, if he was agreeable to it.

Now I just had to convince Sir Jonas himself.

A tall, lanky gentleman paused in the doorframe, then bumped his sword hilt against a circular wooden table as he pushed the door partway shut. His hasty bow tipped the lantern perched atop the table, nearly sending it careening to the floor.

I fought a wince, instead trying for a warm smile. "Please, come in." *Before you break something.*

"Princess." The man hurried forward, then dipped into another unsteady bow. His shoulders drooped a bit at his perusal of my face. "Princess...Liesel, of course."

I tipped my head in acknowledgement. "You are correct. And you must be Sir Jonas."

"Yes, my apologies for failing to make a proper introduction. It's a pleasure to make your acquaintance." He pressed my offered hand, shifting his weight from foot to foot. "For a moment, I thought you might be... That is, you look very like your sister. But, then, that was years ago."

"Indeed." Hopefully, I wasn't imagining the fondness on his face at the mention of Verena. "I have been told many times I resemble a younger version of the Crown Princess."

"Of course." He passed a hand over his sword hilt, sending the sheath crashing against his leg.

"Let's sit and get comfortable." I beckoned to the chairs grouped around the large stone fireplace and dropped into one. Perhaps this poor man would finally relax if he sat down.

"I thank you, Princess Liesel." He backed into one chair before folding his long frame into another. "Lord Hamelun said you wanted to speak with me, but I wasn't sure—"

"Yes, I appreciate that you've taken the time to meet with me." I took a deep breath. *This is your chance, Liesel.* This miserable journey could not go to waste. "I've come to ask you to return with us to Telynn Castle."

His eyes widened, his fingers stilling on the loose thread he'd been fiddling with. "Return? You may not be aware, Princess, but it was at the behest of your father that I came to Ormande. I'm not sure—"

"I am aware, but circumstances have changed. There has been...trouble with Markou. We aren't certain the extent of it yet, but it is clear they are plotting. Trying to infiltrate our borders." *There, nothing about that was dishonest.* "Sir Ennoh specifically noted your loyalty to the royal family during your time with us. You are just the sort of dedicated knight that we need to rely upon while we sort out any treachery from Markou."

"Sir Ennoh said that? About me?" He sat up straighter, his lips curving in a hopeful smile.

At last, a glimpse of what might've drawn Verena to this gangly fellow. His face, though too angular to be considered traditionally handsome, held an earnestness, a steadfast kindness that must've endeared him to Verena's sensitive nature. His blond hair was cropped close, as though it were the one aspect of his body he could control with precision. The blue of his uniform accentuated his wide blue eyes.

"He did." I nodded with a smile full of encouragement. "He praised your honesty and dedication to your position."

Sir Jonas relaxed against the back of his chair. "It's not easy to earn Sir Ennoh's respect, that's for certain. It means a lot to hear he saw my good qualities alongside..." He swallowed, ducking his head.

No need to bring up the poor man's clumsiness. "So I'm here to recruit you, if you're willing. Lord Hamelun has already granted his permission, but the decision is up to you. If you have a family you don't want to leave, or..." *You mustn't already have a wife and children!*

He slapped his knee. "Nothing tying me down in that respect, Princess. Not many ladies to be met this far into the mountains."

I could've hugged him for that shy, sheepish grin. *Please have lingering feelings for Verena that can be rekindled.*

"I'm prepared to serve the royal family in whatever task you need. Of course I'll join you." He rose, nearly tripping as he unfolded his legs. "Shall we depart right away?"

"In the morning, I think." I stood as well, striving to keep my smile welcoming rather than smug. "Let's find the other members of my party to prepare."

"I'll need to get Lord Hamelun's approval to take a mount, but I'm certain he won't object for a royal mission." Sir Jonas was listing the preparations he'd need to make as we neared the sitting room where Breck and Nadette supposedly waited.

I winced at the grand vision he'd apparently conjured around the need for his presence at Telynn Castle. Then the rest of his comment struck me. "Even with Lord Hamelun's consent, I'm not sure you'll be able to bring an elk."

He turned to me, a question in his eyes.

"I'm afraid we had to leave ours behind almost two days ago." I pushed away the fears for Tassie that threatened to plague my thoughts. "There was a ledge—"

"Ah, you took the Aaren Pass." He nodded, his expression pensive. "The shortest way here from Telynn Castle, I suppose, but trickier terrain."

"Tricky, indeed." Though I couldn't deny I was looking forward to encountering that cliff face again. The way down was sure to be even more exhilarating. "Let's discuss it with the others."

As if on cue, the servant leading us paused at a doorway. There were so many in this fortress, and each hall seemed to look exactly the same. Narrow and utilitarian, but with a decorative etching on each wooden door. "I believe you will find your companions within." She hovered uncertainly, clearly not used to hosting visitors.

"Thank you." I nodded at her and hurried inside. In contrast to the darkness of the halls, this room had tall windows boasting a stunning view of the mountainside. *Perhaps there was a good reason for living this far north after all.*

Breck and Nadette stood from their fur-lined chairs.

I couldn't hold back a grin as their curious gazes moved to the knight following behind me. "Lady Nadette, Sir Albrecht, I'd like to introduce you to Sir Jonas. He's agreed to accompany us back to Telynn Castle."

Nadette extended her hand with a warm welcome. "How good of you to join us, Sir Jonas."

Breck paused at my side, his low murmur grazing my ear. "Well done. And you even remembered my full name."

I shrugged. "We haven't been traveling *that* long." Though it felt like an eternity.

After Breck and Sir Jonas exchanged brief greetings, I motioned for everyone to take a seat. I sank into my chair, the fur lining scratchy but warm.

"Sir Jonas and I were just discussing a potential setback for our return trip. If he brings his own elk, we won't be able to take the same route. But if we try to circumvent that cliff face, we'd lose a lot of time."

Breck leaned forward. "Even more to regain our own elk."

"Exactly. I'm not leaving Tassie behind." I looked between Breck and Sir Jonas. "There's no closer way around it? Nowhere an elk could...jump down?"

Both men shook their heads. Sir Jonas gripped the arm of his chair. "Not without risking a broken leg, or worse."

"Princess?" Nadette raised her timid voice. "Tassie would suit Sir Jonas well enough for a few days' journey, don't you think? You're very welcome to join me on Hilde."

Breck gave her a kind smile. "I'm afraid Hilde is too small to manage two riders. But you have the right idea. Tassie would do well for Sir Jonas."

He threaded his fingers together, his expression changing to...amusement? Uncertainty? "Princess Liesel will ride with me."

"You?" My exclamation came out as much squawk as question. "Why couldn't you and Sir Jonas ride together on Klaus? Or—"

"Sir Jonas and I would be too heavy a combination to ride one mount." His voice held a grating note of patience, as though explaining to a child why she can't have more sweets. "And both of us are too tall to ride little Hilde, otherwise you and Lady Nadette might've been able to share Tassie."

I crossed my arms with a huff. "Surely there must be some other—"

He raised his brows. "Do you want to get Sir Jonas to Telynn Castle or not?"

"Yes, fine." My glare turned mischievous. "At least I have the next two days of walking to dream up songs to hum. Or, perhaps, I'll see how many of Sir Ennoh's jokes I can recall."

Sir Jonas gave a nervous chuckle.

Breck groaned and buried his head in his hands. "Holy One, give me patience."

I relaxed further into my chair. "You know, the best way to gain a skill is to practice it."

"Plenty of practice these days," Breck muttered before raising his eyes heavenward. "And help me to somehow keep this one out of trouble until she's returned to the king and queen."

"Well, you must be quite proud of yourself, Princess." Breck crouched to pick up a stick.

We'd departed in the morning and made the trek through the rock-strewn Aaren Pass in a drizzly fog. Fortunately, without incident. The rain had stopped, but the clouds seemed thicker than ever as darkness approached. Breck and I were scouring the woods for as much dry firewood as we could carry, while Nadette and Sir Jonas prepared our campsite.

I shot him a grin. "I'm proud of myself for a great many things. Which do you happen to be speaking of this time?"

He grunted. "I haven't had a chance to commend you for your success with Sir Jonas. I know you can be persuasive—or, at least, pesky—but I wasn't sure even you could convince a guard who'd been sent away from the castle to return years later in a gamble to wed your sister."

"It's true, no one's more pesky than I." I bent to peer at the damp ground, enveloped by an earthy scent. "Didn't we agree that it would be safer for you to call me Liesel?"

He shook his head. "You making a suggestion hardly counts as an agreement, though you're proving my point quite admirably. Peskiness isn't often a trait to be admired, but in this case I must confess congratulations are in order."

"Thank you." My tone was bright, but guilt nagged my conscience. My feat wasn't nearly as impressive as he likely thought.

He chuckled, a warm, soothing sound. "Sir Jonas is a braver man than I. It would be challenge enough to face your father and the other guards who knew of his dismissal. Then to be expected to do something ridiculous to make Princess Verena laugh? He must've really come to admire your sister."

The edges of my lips felt strung tight. "She makes a lasting impression, I guess."

Breck dropped an armload of sticks onto our pile with a clatter. "Is something wrong? You should be grinning with a smug 'I told you so,' not deflecting with short, vague responses." He stepped closer. "Did Sir Jonas say something to upset you? Do you think he won't be a good match for your sister after all?"

I rose, snagging my hair on a low branch. "Nothing of the sort. Sir Jonas has been all kindness and cordiality and would suit Verena very well, I think.

Perhaps in convincing him to accompany us, I used up all my persuasive powers for a time. Such a talent isn't without cost, you know."

"Hmm. It doesn't quite fit." He pressed his lips together. "When you accomplish feats of persuasion on me, it seems to give you energy rather than depleting it."

I gave my hair a stronger tug as I disentangled it from the twig. "When have I ever persuaded you of anything?"

"I came along without alerting your parents, didn't I?" He circled to face me, trying to meet my gaze. "Wait. Is Sir Jonas actually aware of the reason we fetched him, or did you give him some alternate excuse?"

I suppressed a growl. How did this man read me so well? And why did he feel the need to call me Princess, yet never hesitate to point out my every fault?

A heavy sigh shook his shoulders. "That's why you're not more pleased with yourself. He's only coming with us because you lied to him. Or gave him a royal command."

With a final yank, I set my hair free. "I did neither." My tone quieted as I remembered Sir Jonas himself was nearby. "But all your sarcasm and logic made me doubt my original plan. I worried if I came on too strong, he'd refuse to join us without giving it a second thought. So instead of overwhelming him with every detail right at the start, I merely told him he was needed at the castle by the royal family. Which is very true."

"*What?*" His whisper held more ire than a shout. "You failed to mention that he'll have to make a fool of himself when he arrives at the castle? That he would be *marrying the Crown Princess of Walthar* should your plan succeed? How could you abuse his loyalty to the kingdom by making him think his services are needed, when in reality his presence is merely missed by your lovesick sister? Who hasn't even seen him in seven years?"

I flinched at his insensitive description of Verena. "I never said she was lovesick. She—"

"Why else would you traipse about the countryside searching for this man? Even you wouldn't be that reckless for less."

My jaw stiffened. "Be careful how you speak of your Crown Princess."

Anger etched lines into his temples. "Crown Princess or not, it's not fair to make this man leave his home and trek across the countryside for days under false pretenses, only to be confused and humiliated when we arrive."

I blinked back the tears that threatened to make me look like a child in the face of his disapproval. "I didn't spend nearly as much time with him as Verena did, but you forget that I knew Sir Jonas when he was a guard at Telynn Castle. He was devoted to my sister and often made himself look foolish in order to draw a smile or laugh from her. I mentioned Verena when I spoke with him, and he still seems to harbor a fondness for her. So you're the one who's being unfair in assuming I hadn't thought any of this through." With a tremulous breath, I took a step back. "Of course I plan to tell him before we arrive at the castle. I just thought I'd allow him to slowly warm to the idea rather than douse him with it all at once."

His tight jaw worked, as though holding back another tirade. "I'll make sure you do." With a parting glare and lurching movements, he lifted an armful of kindling.

"I'll finish gathering on my own." The last word came out as a sob as I fled farther into the tree cover.

Chapter 8

My blistered feet protested every step. Up rises, down steep descents, through forests smelling of pine and freesia. Down the cliff face with ropes and many squeals of alarm from Nadette. No one had attempted to injure me or hinder our journey, and only light spring rains had slowed us down.

Now, finally, the clearing where we'd left the elk was up ahead. I was going to hug dear Tassie tighter than I ever had before.

As though feeling a similar sense of exhaustion mixed with anticipation, Nadette and Sir Jonas fell silent as we veered off the path. Just past these bushes and the swaying daphne flowers, into the cluster of fir trees.

I strained to hear a grunt or stomp of hooves, but only birdsong and swishing grasses met my ears. *Hopefully they're not in distress, then, just relaxed and...*

We crossed through the barrier of thick spiny branches, and my thoughts drifted away like the fluffy white seeds blowing in the breeze. The little round meadow we'd selected so carefully for its combination of food, water, and shade, was empty.

"Tassie? Tassie!" I winced at the rising pitch of my voice. "Where are they?"

My companions circled the clearing, looking as bewildered as I felt.

Nadette frowned up at the long branches with their dark cones. "We didn't have a clear path to follow. Perhaps these clearings all look the same, and we ended up in the wrong one."

"Not possible." Breck shook his head, his tone gentle but firm. "The grass here has been trampled by large animals."

"Did you have them tied over here?" Sir Jonas lifted a scrap of rope that still clung to one of the trees.

I suppressed a shudder. Clamped down on the desire to run, shouting, through the forest in a desperate search for my elk. "Do you think they ran away? Or—?" I couldn't complete the statement, even in my mind.

"Looks more like they were set free." Sir Jonas ran a thumb over the coarse rope. "Someone cut through this with a knife."

"Or stolen." Breck had joined Sir Jonas's inspection. "They must've been able to untie the other ropes."

Hopefully alive, then. I clung to that thread of hope.

"Who would've done such a thing?" Nadette fiddled with the fringe of her shawl. "Oh, gracious, I do hope they're all right."

Scanning the ground, I located trampled grass opposite the direction we'd come. "They must've gone this way. Let's find them." I set out, not bothering to check whether anyone followed.

If Tassie was out there somewhere, either alone or in the hands of thieves, I had to find her.

"Princess." Breck caught up to me and cupped his hand around my elbow. "Regardless of how they came untied, the elk could be long gone. We may not be able to locate them."

"No. We have to find them."

"That would be my preference as well, of course. But if we can't track down our elk, we can cut through Borghne on our return journey. It's only a few days away, and I'm sure we can find new mounts to purchase or at least borrow." With one last squeeze, he let go of my arm. "We won't have to walk the entire way back, I promise."

"I don't care about walking." *Not that I want to.* Before panic could tighten my voice, I took several deep breaths and pasted on a smile. "It's just that Tassie is accustomed to being the preferred mount of a princess and has long been treated as such. She is surely less than pleased about roaming the woods with no one to care for her, or with the rough treatment she'd receive at the hands of a petty thief."

Breck narrowed his eyes, apparently not fooled by the haughty tilt of my head. "We'll do everything we can to find her, Liesel. I promise."

I poked another stick into the fire. *Why, when I've seen Breck build half a dozen fires, can I not get these embers to reignite?*

"What are you doing?" Breck's shadow darkened the fire circle.

"Good morning." I spared him a glance before prodding the fire again. "May I use your dagger? I don't want to get mine dirty. And why isn't this fire cooperating?"

"If that stick was on the ground, it's likely damp. This might work better." He peeled loose bark from the nearest tree and handed it to me. "But we should be extinguishing the fire if we're going to resume our search for the elk."

I inched the bark into the glowing embers and was rewarded with a spark. "Not yet. First, I need to roast these apples."

"Apples?" Breck blinked and rubbed his eyes.

"Yes, I found an apple tree back near the path." I waved my left arm vaguely, my eyes on the growing flame. "That's why I need your dagger."

His already furrowed brows lowered further. "But why do you need to roast them?"

"They're delicious." I tipped my head back to regard him. "Haven't you ever had roasted apples? With cinnamon or nutmeg?"

"I...I've had them, when I was a child."

"Your dagger, please." I held out my open palm.

Gingerly, as though handing a sword to a young boy, he placed the handle into my waiting fingers. "To slice the apples, I suppose?"

I nodded. "Certainly, now you're catching on. Do you always struggle so much in the morning?"

If his cough covered a mumbled complaint, I chose to ignore it. "But do you really need roasted apples on a morning we're in a hurry? Couldn't you just eat the apples fresh?"

"They're so much better roasted. But they're not for me." I shifted my weight on my sore legs.

"They're not." This time he rubbed his forehead, as though already developing a headache.

"Tassie loves roasted apples." Just saying her name stabbed me with a pang of remorse. "I'm hoping if she's anywhere nearby, she might smell them and come closer."

"Ah." His face cleared for an instant before puckering again. "You feed your elk roasted apples?"

I shrugged. "She likes them as much as I do."

"Of course she does." He shook his head with a grumbling laugh. "Only a princess."

Riled by his tone, I attacked the apple in my hand with vigor. "I couldn't think of what else to do. With so little trail to follow, and no sign of them last night..."

"Last night?" Breck crouched to peer into my face. "Did you sleep at all?"

"A little." I sniffed, smirking in satisfaction when a drop of juice landed on his cheek. "But I didn't want to miss anything if Tassie made a sound during the night. You know...in distress, or looking for me."

His expression softened, and he patted my shoulder before rising back to his full height. "We'll find her, Princess. Enjoy your apples."

My voice hardly functioned anymore, but I croaked out her name again. "Tassie!" We'd been searching the woods for hours, and I could tell by Breck's defeated expression that he considered our elk lost for good. But I refused to give up. My beloved girl had to be nearby, and I wouldn't abandon her.

"Milady, you're working yourself into a right state." Nadette gave my arm a sympathetic squeeze, her tone conciliatory. "Do you think, perhaps, the elk were able to sense the path home? If we head in that direction, we might catch up with them. Or find them safe on the castle grounds, tucked into their stalls."

I shook my head. "What if you're wrong? We can't give up yet."

"I know how much you care for Tassie, Princess. But, gracious, if we don't make any forward progress today, I'm afraid—"

"Listen." I stilled. Perhaps my tired mind was playing tricks on me, but that snuffle sounded just like... I broke into a run, overcome by the need to test my theory before my hope could rise far enough to cause permanent damage when it crashed.

"Milady, wait! If the thieves are still afoot..." Nadette took off after me, but her shorter legs couldn't keep up.

"Tassie, is that you?" Twigs scraped my arms, and I yanked my skirt from the clutches of a thorny bush.

Ahead, a russet head turned from inspecting the bark of a tree, ears high and alert.

"Tassie!" I threw my arms around her neck, pulling fuzz-covered slices of roasted apple from my pack. She nuzzled my face and hair with a playful chirp.

"I saved these for you, girl."

She licked my thumb before closing her lips around the treat.

"Milady?" Nadette's hurried steps crinkled through the brush behind me. "Oh! Praise the Holy One, you really did find her. I'll go tell the others."

I stroked Tassie's back as she finished her last apple slice. "Are your friends nearby, dear girl? Klaus and Hilde?" Her ears perked up at the names. "Can you take me to them?"

She broke into a trot, and I laughed, jogging at her side. *Thank you, Holy One, for not letting her be injured or stolen or irretrievably lost.*

"Princess Liesel?" Breck's shout made a pair of black birds squawk and take flight from a nearby branch.

"Over here." I wasn't about to stop and wait for him.

Tassie made a high chirp, and a haunting keen answered to our left.

"That must be Klaus. Smart girl." I scratched under her ear as Klaus crashed through the underbrush toward us. "Good to see you, friend." I patted him with a grin.

A whine sounded just ahead. Hopefully Hilde on her way. "You stayed together, you took care of each other. Well done." I'd make sure each one would receive their fill of roasted apples for years to come.

"There you are, Princess." Breck halted behind me, eyes wide. "You found...all of them."

"I told you they must've remained in these woods." My tone was too relieved to manage a show of superiority. "And I'm so glad I was right." I returned to Tassie's side, slinging an arm across her neck.

Never again would I leave her behind.

"As am I. Though I still don't understand—if someone set them free, why wouldn't they keep them, or…" He let his words trail off with a shrug. "I guess I'm glad they didn't, whatever their motivation. If there even was a person involved." He patted Klaus and ran a hand along his lead rope. "I'm starting to see the benefits of your dogged perseverance."

"It's about time." Meeting his warm gaze, I took Hilde's severed lead line. "Let's get you back to Nadette, little one."

Nadette and Sir Jonas expressed equal joy and surprise at our discovery. My own relief was only marred by the nagging question of how they'd gotten free in the first place. Had Breck's knots really been so feeble? Had they been fleeing a predator? Or was Sir Jonas right that someone set them free? Another perusal of my mount provided assurance she was unhurt.

Whatever had befallen them, they were safe now.

Breck was already draping a blanket across Klaus's thick shoulders and digging for extra rope. Within minutes, he'd swung up onto Klaus's back. "If we depart now, we can make use of the last few hours of daylight. Princess?" He extended a hand to me.

Drat. I'd nearly forgotten the annoyance of needing to ride with Breck in my panic over the missing elk. But to reignite the argument would only waste more time. Giving Tassie one last squeeze, I relinquished her to Sir Jonas.

"I'll take good care of her, Princess." He accepted her newly-tied lead line with a smile.

"I'm sure you will." I believed it, too—as long as he didn't accidentally poke her with his sword or fall off trying to reach a handful of mulberries.

Facing Breck once more, I scowled but took his hand as I placed my foot in the curved strap sewn into the side of Klaus's blanket. Thank goodness the bull's new spring antlers had only recently sprouted. How anyone could enjoy riding with a towering rack of spikes on either side of their mount's head was beyond me.

Breck chuckled. "Come now, don't the most exciting stories always involve a princess being swept away on a knight's valiant steed?"

I adjusted my riding stance to fit Klaus's width. "Why in the snows would she want to do that when she has a perfectly good steed of her own?"

His arms surrounded me on either side as he flicked the reins. "Clearly most princesses don't come as prepared as you."

"Clearly." I held my back stiff as Klaus ambled forward, determined *not* to act like the princesses in the romantic stories he referenced. "And don't forget this was *your* idea. Perhaps you just wanted a closer look at my *distinctive* dark hair."

Another laugh shook his chest. "Perhaps. If nothing else, it will give me an opportunity to remove some of the debris that has accumulated from all our nights sleeping on the ground."

"Debris?" A hint of concern undermined my playful tone.

His fingers pinched my hair in several places, then reached forward to dispose of a twig and several leaves.

I tried to summon indignation, but instead an odd tingle seeped from my scalp down my back. "Ah, yes. I thought I'd try more of a woodland princess look. After all, I didn't bring any of my jeweled pins along."

Instead of the expected snort, he made a thoughtful hum. "You know, I think you ought to forgo the jeweled pins altogether. This look suits you better."

The hive's worth of bees that began buzzing around my midsection must've been from hunger. Or perhaps Klaus's unfamiliar gait.

Nothing to do with the idea that Breck might find me attractive, twigs and all.

"Lean back, Princess."

The sudden command jolted me upright. How long had we been riding? An hour? Two? "No, thank you."

"Liesel." Breck's tone softened, his breath ruffling the hair at my ear. "I know you're exhausted after a long night fretting about Tassie. But if you fall forward, you'll spook Klaus and may end up trampled on the ground. If you lean against me, you can rest in safety."

My spine tightened. Despite the necessity of sharing the same mount, I'd continued to avoid contact with Breck as much as possible. "How weak you must think me."

"I think your strength has been tested far beyond anything you've been prepared for. That you care so much about your elk that you wouldn't allow yourself to sleep in case you missed a sign of her. But look." He pointed ahead of us on the path. "Tassie is alive and well, and Sir Jonas hasn't even toppled off yet. Now you can finally get some rest."

I stifled a yawn.

"Please." His whisper was in my ear again. "Don't let your pride cause you to get hurt."

My sigh huffed out a bit more dramatically than necessary. "Fine. Just for a little while." I eased back, part relieved and part annoyed that I fit so comfortably against him.

He shifted until my head drooped against his shoulder, then secured an arm around my waist. "Sweet dreams." He murmured the words so close to my hair that I felt more than heard them.

If the smile in his tone was meant to be teasing, I was too tired to protest. Warm, secure, and as comfortable as one could get astride a massive elk, I let Klaus's swaying rhythm lull me to sleep.

Chapter 9

I REMOVED ANOTHER BURR from Tassie's coat. The poor girl must've found quite the patch of bramble in her wanderings. The others were bedding down for the night, but I'd needed something to ease my restlessness before I could join them.

"I hope you're planning to sleep soon." Breck crept up beside me, his face aglow in the light of the full moon.

"Soon. You needn't wait up." He'd been a perfect gentleman the past day and a half while I'd ridden Klaus with him. Teasing and at times grumpy, of course, but nothing to set Nadette's propriety-loving heart ill at ease. Our physical contact had been minimal, under the circumstances.

Except when I slept against him. The memory brought the heat of embarrassment thrumming up my neck, along with something...else. A strange tug that made me want to both find an excuse to lean against him again and stay as far from him as possible.

I shook away the unsettling thoughts, giving him a tight-lipped smile.

"Do you need any help?" Was it only the moonlight that made his gaze so soft?

"No, thank you." I ducked to Tassie's other side and ran the brush across her coarse fur, drawing calm from her steady warmth. "I groom her myself even at the castle. I enjoy the time with her. Especially now, after…"

"I understand. The two of you have an admirable bond. I'm sorry to interrupt." He patted Tassie's side. "But I wanted to ask how it went earlier."

My movements stilled. "How what went?"

"With Sir Jonas. At the fire." His brows were raised in expectation. Eagerness, even.

I willed my expression not to show my inner consternation. "He…showed me a few tricks for lighting the fire. I think I'm improving." Somehow I doubted I was answering his true question.

His chuckle was practically a snort. "You certainly did need help with that particular task." He leaned closer, his low voice conspiratorial. "But your conversation. He's still with us, so he at least must be taking your plan under consideration."

Oh dear. What made him think we'd discussed that subject? I stooped to brush down Tassie's legs. And perhaps to avoid his gaze. He'd been dropping hints and giving me meaningful glances every time I strayed near Sir Jonas, but… "I don't believe Sir Jonas knows any more of my plan than he did before."

"What?" He glanced behind us, likely to see if his harsh tone had awakened our sleeping companions. "He still isn't aware of your father's proclamation?" He lowered his voice again, this time to a growl. "He doesn't know that he's being led to your lovelorn sister and will be expected to marry her?"

Tassie snuffed as I tugged too hard at a knot. "Of course I'm still planning to tell him. But why did it have to be at that exact moment?"

"I joined Lady Nadette's berry picking to give you time alone with him." Breck pushed tense fingers through his hair. "We'll arrive at Telynn Castle in two days. Will you feign shock at the contest for your sister's hand? Beg your father to dream up some pretense for requiring Sir Jonas's presence? You're running out of time, Princess."

"No...I know." Much as I hated to agree with him, the refrain had been on my mind all day. *Almost home. Almost home.* "You're right, that would've been a good opportunity. I'm sorry I didn't realize it at the time."

Breck sighed, his expression softening. "I want to support your efforts here. Truly. But I can't condone blindly leading a good man into a situation that would no doubt cause him to be embarrassed and overwhelmed. He must be prepared for what you expect of him."

Nodding, I rose from my crouch. "I—"

A rustle in the bushes cut off my words.

The brush clattered from my hand. "What was that?"

"A startled animal?" Breck was on alert, scanning the hedge.

I sidled against Tassie. "It sounded awfully big for an animal. Do we need to be concerned about some creature out hunting? Or some*one* who—" I wasn't sure how best to complete the phrase, but he seemed to catch my meaning.

"I'll go investigate. Please, join the others as soon as you can." He bent into the briefest of bows before jogging in the direction of the sound.

Were the running footsteps his, someone else's, or a figment of my imagination?

"I'll find a way to tell Sir Jonas, somehow." I leaned my forehead against Tassie's neck. "Thanks for never lecturing me, dear girl." She snuffled against my shoulder. "And if you sense anyone prowling tonight, squeal as loudly as you can."

I squeezed excess water from my hair as I climbed the rise from the stream back to where we'd camped. Nice as it felt to be relatively clean, I couldn't wait to truly scrub off every last speck of dirt in a warm bath once we returned to the castle. *Nearly there.*

The thought didn't bring as much relief as I'd expected. While the comforts of home would be heavenly, what would happen to the teasing camaraderie I'd developed with Breck along our journey? Then again, perhaps it was already gone since he still seemed distant after our argument the night before.

My stomach tightened with more than hunger. *Only two days to find a way to tell Sir Jonas—*

A stick cracked nearby, jarring my thoughts. "Nadette? Feel free to freshen up in the stream. I'm on my way to—"

"You aren't on your way anywhere, little miss." A hand closed around my upper arm, gripping so tight I could feel each fingertip bruise my skin.

I whirled to see the man who had materialized at my side. Tall and lean, with short-cropped dark hair. And a sikha juice tattoo marking the back of his left hand.

"Unhand me at once, you brute." I shoved against him before stomping on the toe of his boot. "Breck! Sir—"

"That's enough of that, *Princess.*" He spat the word like an oath as he slapped his free hand over my mouth, using my arm to drag me parallel to the stream.

I tried to bite his hand, but he kept his palm curved away from my teeth. My feet couldn't find purchase on the dew-moistened grass, but my flailing fist landed blows to his shoulder and chin.

He cursed and removed his hand from my mouth.

I gasped an inhale, but before I could scream, something cold and sharp pricked my collarbone. I stilled, struggling to control my breathing.

"That's more like it. No more fighting, no more yelling. I'd hate to have to deliver you with scars marring that pretty face and neck." He trailed the knife point up my jaw.

My teeth ground together in an attempt to contain my shudder. "Deliver me where?"

"The fine kingdom of Markou." He repositioned himself behind me and shoved me forward. "His Highness, Prince Carre, tires of unsuccessful negotiations with Walthar."

I shuffled forward, mind racing. Breck and the others would miss me soon. They'd never let this buffoon take me all the way to Markou. I just had to stall, distract him.

Maybe aggravate him.

"I believe I spotted a tattoo on your hand. You were one of the masked suitors, then? I suspected your prince planned to claim Verena if any of you succeeded. Too cowardly to try for her himself, I assume?"

"Prince Carre is no coward." His voice was a growl at my ear. "No one of royal blood could be expected to demean himself in such a way, just to entertain your shrew of a sister."

I pressed my lips together. *Not the time to lose your temper, Liesel.* "He just let his servants do it for him. Were you the one who marched around to his own orders? Or maybe the juggler? The ventriloquist? Of course, nothing you did to try to make my sister laugh could've been half as demeaning as kidnapping a princess."

He grunted, pressing the blade closer to my throat.

"Does Prince Carre even know you're doing this?" Another attempt at digging my heels into the ground failed as he dragged me onward. "Holding me hostage or marrying me by force is hardly a promising start to an alliance."

"It's time for Markou to be done waiting around for an alliance. Done kowtowing to an inferior kingdom." An elk snuffled ahead.

Hope flared in my chest, until an unfamiliar charcoal-fading-to-gray coat came into view. I fought to relax my tensing muscles. *Time for more distractions.*

"You're by yourself? I thought at least you'd have a company of failed look-alike suitors."

He scoffed. "I'm making all the effort, I'll get all the glory. I may have failed as a suitor, but I'm the one who spotted you leaving with just your maidservant and caught wind of your plan. At first, I thought merely to turn you back, thwart your journey. But now...just think how Prince Carre will reward me for surprising him with a Waltharian princess right at his doorstep."

No others to worry about, then. Little wonder his attempts had been sporadic and small in scale. "You honestly expect to drag me all the way to Markou without getting caught? I'm certain my companions have missed me already and will be here any moment to..."

His dark chuckle sent a shiver up my spine. "I somehow doubt that."

An entirely new set of fears bubbled in my chest, a pot of boiling water ready to overflow. Heedless of the dagger, I spun to face him. "What did you do to them?"

"It's a shame about the fire. That Jonas fellow is so very clumsy, he must've kicked a burning twig. No doubt your poor maidservant fainted at the very sight of it." He shrugged, with a smile that might've been handsome if not for the cruel gleam in his eyes.

Black spots danced across my vision. *Fire?* They needed my help, and I was about to be carried off on an elk to who knew what fate.

Protect them, Holy One. And me.

A whisper floated into my consciousness, as much a presence as a word. *Always.*

The reassurance sent a thread of peace through my panic, calming my racing mind enough to think. My captor hauled me up onto his mount in front of him, but I didn't waste energy protesting.

Time to come up with a plan.

I patted the elk's soft neck and leaned as far forward as my captor's grip allowed. Noting the lack of antlers, I murmured in my gentlest tone, "That's a good girl. I'm sorry you're stuck with this one for a master. I'll try to free you if I can."

"Gallop, Argele." The Unmasked Bandit barked the command and snapped the reins, but the elk hesitated.

I scratched between her ears, resuming my whispering. "Argele? What a lovely name. Listen to him for now. I'll let you know when it's time to listen to me."

"Leave her be." He hauled me against his chest with an arm around my waist. Nothing like Breck's gentle strength. But between holding me steady and his grip on the reins, I no longer felt the icy pinprick of the dagger.

I gave Argele a reassuring pat before straightening my spine. She stumbled forward with a whine, adjusting to the weight of two riders.

After several more snaps of the reins, my captor seemed to accept that a second rider meant a slower pace.

I scanned our surroundings, looking for my opportunity. Trying not to picture the danger my travel companions might be facing as they struggled to put out a fire.

An open, rocky plateau appeared ahead. *Perfect.* I flexed my fingers in my lap, giving the elk the slightest pressure with my legs. *Three...two...one.*

We entered the clearing, and I shouted "Turn!" while pressing my heel into Argele's right side. Grasping the reins with one hand, I scratched at my captor's arm and shoved when he loosened his grip. He lost his balance and fell as we pivoted in the opposite direction.

"That's it, girl. Perfect." I bent low, giving her neck a quick pat. "Now run!"

But Bandit was already on his feet. He grasped my leg before we could make our escape, getting dragged as the elk started back toward our campsite.

I shrieked, the fabric of my skirt tearing as he launched himself back on.

Poor Argele squeaked her protest as I kicked and shoved at our unwanted passenger.

"Liesel?" Breck's panicked shout sounded ahead.

"Breck!" I didn't even mind that my relieved cry made it sound like he was my favorite person in the world.

At the moment, I had to admit he was.

He rode up on Klaus, face pained and sooty, hair disheveled. Never had a knight looked so noble and brave.

Bandit used my distraction to position himself behind me, yanking my hair as he tried to take back the reins.

"Unhand the princess at once." Breck pulled Klaus to a halt before us and drew his sword.

"Very watchful of the princess, aren't you?" Bandit sneered, not nearly as alarmed by this development as I'd hoped. "Pulled her away from my landslide, found her precious elk, and it's taken me days to catch her alone. My efforts won't go unrewarded." He reached around me, and a prick nipped at the front of my neck.

Not the knife again. I kept my shoulders steady as my spirits sagged. Breck would feel powerless to act if he felt it might compromise my safety.

His eyes widened, and his sword lowered to his side.

"That's right, *Breck*. I'd hate to have to injure the princess because of your hasty actions." Bandit's chest puffed out—if he were on the ground, the irritating fop would've been strutting. "Now, to ensure her ongoing safety, I need you to return to your king. Tell him his daughter jumped at the opportunity to make an advantageous marriage and will be well cared for." He coughed. "As long as everyone cooperates, that is."

Breck's gaze flickered between Bandit's knife and the surrounding trees. Together we could take on this power-hungry Markan, but how could we form and communicate a plan? I couldn't urge Argele forward when she'd crash headlong into Klaus.

"Not so brave and haughty now, are you?" Bandit brandished the knife. "We'll be on our way, but just remember—"

His words choked off in a strangled cry as he slumped forward and toppled from Argele's back.

My gasp turned into a laugh at the sight of Sir Jonas on a stump behind us, wielding a large rock.

He shrugged. "My aim isn't too bad at close range."

Breck's tense expression broke into a grin. "Well done, friend." He sheathed his sword, dismounted Klaus, and jogged forward to clap Sir Jonas on the back.

When he turned to me, the intensity of his gaze melted my thoughts to slush. "Liesel? Are you hurt?"

I swallowed. *Bandit is down, no more need for a racing pulse.* "Only injured pride that the fool managed to pull his dagger on me a second time." I dismounted, landing right at Breck's feet. Torn between jumping away and throwing my arms around him, I awkwardly patted his shoulder. "I'm well, thanks to you."

His amber eyes never left mine. *Breathe, Liesel.*

Retreating a step to give Argele a pat, I glanced to Sir Jonas. "Thanks to both of you."

His smile held a hint of...suspicion? Amusement? "I'm grateful we found you in time, Princess Liesel. And that I managed to be useful in protecting a member of the royal family before we even reached the castle."

Guilt nudged my chest at his glowing pride. "But are you well? Nadette? He mentioned a fire, and I was so worried…"

"That explains it." Breck directed a glare at the fallen Bandit. "I knew we hadn't left burning embers."

Sir Jonas set down his rock. "Lady Nadette is unhurt. We lost a blanket and will need to replenish our water supply, but no real harm was done."

Breck nodded. "We should only have one night left on the road, so I'm not concerned. Lady Nadette wasn't injured by the fire, but she's likely in a panic over your disappearance."

"Oh dear, I'm sure you're right." The sweet woman wasn't going to let me out of her sight for days.

"Let's get this ruffian back to camp where we can properly tie him up." Breck crouched and hauled Bandit up beneath his arms.

"I'm sure Argele here would be happy to give him a ride, now that he can no longer strike her with the reins." I stroked the beautiful animal's cheek. "I think she and Tassie will get along just fine."

Chapter 10

"Sir Jonas?" My voice threatened to squeak.

We'd found a cave in which to spend the night and sat huddled around a fire just outside the entrance. Poor Sir Jonas had a bandage wrapped around two fingers that had been burned in his attempt to put out the fire.

Even with Breck and Nadette as an audience, it was high time I let him know the true reason he was on this quest. With the way Nadette had fretted over me since the attempted kidnapping, it was unlikely I'd ever get a moment alone with the man, anyway.

"Yes?" He jumped to his feet, clearly still on edge. He coughed, his cheeks flushing pink. "Sorry, Princess Liesel. I just... What did you need?" He lowered himself back to the ground, his chagrined smile still brimming with his usual good nature.

"I apologize for startling you. I think we'll all be a bit jumpy for the next few days." My gaze darted to the surrounding trees, but I forced it back to his earnest face. Sweet Sir Jonas deserved my full attention.

My full honesty.

"After the danger today, I think it's time I explained the real reason I requested your presence at Telynn Castle. Far past time." I tucked a trembling hand beneath my gray skirt.

Breck's brows raised, but he nodded in agreement. Nadette gave me an encouraging smile.

Sir Jonas tilted his head. "Of course, if it would help me better attend to the safety of you and your family."

He was too good. My family didn't deserve such unswerving devotion.

At least, I certainly didn't.

"Thank you. But I'm more concerned about you knowing the full truth." My long inhale made my shoulders quiver. "When you worked at Telynn Castle, you were assigned to guard my sister Verena for a time. No doubt you recall that her disposition is of a rather...melancholy nature."

Sir Jonas's eyes held a hint of fondness. "I used to enjoy finding ways to make her smile."

"She has missed those efforts." I adjusted my position on the hard rock. "In fact, her gloominess in recent years has become so complete that she rarely smiles at all anymore. I can't recall the last time she laughed."

Sir Jonas leaned forward, his expression stricken.

Time to move on to my request. Even Verena wouldn't want him to come back out of pity. "My father is quite distressed that his heir seems miserable so much of the time. It does little to instill confidence in our people, after all."

"I can imagine." Sir Jonas gave a solemn nod.

Now for the tricky part. "As a result, Pappa has declared that Verena must... That he wants to find a gentleman who..."

At my side, Breck cleared his throat.

I pressed my lips together, resisting the urge to direct a glare his way. "He's giving Verena's hand in marriage to the man who can make her laugh." My breath released in a huff.

No turning back now.

Sir Jonas's eyes widened. "That is a drastic step, indeed. And I would imagine quite upsetting to your sister's sensitive nature." His fingers clenched around a jagged stone. "But how could my services as a knight possibly help the situation? And why has it put us in danger?"

I winced. So much for him taking the idea and running with it. "Well, it's not so much your services specifically as a knight that I had in mind. Though your fast thinking and bravery earlier today were exceptional. But the reason I sought you out was that I remembered your ability to...make Verena laugh."

He chuckled. "She certainly did seem to appreciate my antics, but—" His jaw went slack. "You're saying you want me to make her laugh *now*? In order to marry her? And become the future king..." The color drained from his tanned cheeks as he sank back onto his hands.

"I confess that was my hope, yes. I know I should've told you right from the start, but I didn't want to scare you off and thought it would help if you had time to get used to the idea." My words tumbled faster and faster, but I was powerless to stop them. "But now my ridiculous plan has put you in danger and you still didn't even know why, and I want to give you the chance to turn back if you'd prefer." I blinked against the pain to my pride—to my heart—this declaration could cost. "You are under no obligation to continue with us. You never were, and I'm so sorry if my deception caused you to think otherwise."

Sir Jonas rubbed his forehead. "You never ordered me to do anything, Princess Liesel. I'm always happy to help when asked, so please don't concern yourself on that account. But this..." He glanced to where my would-be captor lay tied to a tree. "I still don't understand how this connects to the attack today."

"Markou has long expressed interest in an alliance with Walthar. Most specifically, a marriage alliance." I picked at a loose thread on my skirt. "Our *friend* there confirmed that Prince Carre hoped to use my father's challenge for Verena's hand to his advantage. He sent multiple suitors who bore a resemblance to him, each wearing a mask, to try to make Verena laugh. If any of them succeeded, I'm sure Prince Carre would've attempted to claim the credit."

Partway through my stumbling explanation, Breck had risen and started pacing. Now he paused. "Prince Carre must've suspected something of Princess Liesel's mission when she set out. A number of difficulties crossed our path before we even reached you. We also have reason to believe a conversation of ours on this subject was overheard last evening, which likely prompted today's direct attack." He placed his hand on my head in a gesture so brief I would've thought I imagined it, except for the tingles left behind.

I glanced up. "Actually, he implied he was acting without Prince Carre's knowledge. He claimed to be working alone, perhaps hoping to compensate for his failure to make Verena laugh."

"Ah, so this thug thought to head us off before we reached the castle. Or to kidnap Princess Liesel and use her as leverage." Sir Jonas's usual goofy charm was replaced by the kind of serious expression Breck always wore when discussing official knight business.

"Exactly. Possibly even to encourage Prince Carre to marry her instead of her sister." Breck's brows had never dipped so low, even when he was annoyed with me. "Now that he's been captured, we can only hope he was truly working alone."

A clang brought our attention to the fire, where Nadette had removed a kettle from our supplies. "Gracious, what a clatter." Her round cheeks shone pink in the firelight. "I thought some tea might be nice."

I smiled, my shoulders relaxing. "Excellent idea. Thank you, Nadette."

"We could all use something calming." Breck resumed his seat between myself and Sir Jonas.

Sir Jonas shook his head, his face scrunched in consternation. "But, Princess Liesel, what makes you think I'm so likely to succeed in making your sister laugh where others—many others, it sounds like—have failed? I haven't seen Princess Verena in years, and I am but a lowly guard. One who couldn't serve well enough to keep his place at the castle. Even if I could make her laugh for a moment, I doubt she'd even remember me, let alone want to marry me."

Breck turned to me with raised brows. How much could I say without betraying Verena's confidences?

I pushed a rock toward the fire with the toe of my boot. "She would certainly remember you. She has always spoken of you with great affection. In fact, I believe she was quite...distressed, when Pappa sent you away."

Something like hope seemed to light his gaze before it darkened again. "But such friendly regard hardly equates to a desire to marry someone."

"Not always, but it can make a very promising start. Far better than any stranger from the town or a neighboring kingdom who might succeed in making her laugh. You could even remind her of the time you spent together when you bring your suit. *If* you bring your suit, that is. Then she'd be certain of who you are and could choose to contain her laughter if she truly doesn't want to marry you." I was babbling again, but I *had* to convince him. "But I believe she will want to marry you, or I wouldn't have come all this way just to bring you back to Telynn Castle."

"Here, milady." Nadette pressed a steaming mug into my hands. I took a long inhale of the sweet, earthy smell.

Sir Jonas accepted his mug, keeping his gaze fixed on the fire. "I appreciate your confidence in me. Your idea has merit, but...marriage to the Crown Princess? Fond as I am of Princess Verena, it's a daunting prospect."

"It is." I clenched the handle of my mug like a lifeline. "As I said before, you're under no obligation. If you choose to return to Ormande, you may go with my blessing. We'll even accompany you there, since I'm the one who put you in danger. You should've known the full truth of this quest all along. I realize that now, and I'm so sorry."

Breck's squeeze to my elbow almost made me jump.

"Thank you." Sir Jonas bowed his head over the steam wafting from his tea. "I… I have a lot to consider. I think I'll walk a bit"—he gestured vaguely toward the trees in the distance—"but I won't stray far."

"Of course." I held my smile in place until he disappeared into the shadows before it shattered like a dropped vase.

"Are you all right, Liesel?"

I startled at both Breck's failure to include my title and the gentleness of his tone. "Never better." My lips felt weighted at the edges as I attempted a smile. I'd retreated from the fire into the far end of the oblong cave—the closest I could get to a semblance of privacy.

His brows drew together, forming that line on his forehead that made him appear ten years older. He crouched, then eased down to sit at my side. "I somehow doubt that."

I shrugged. "It's been a trying day, but nothing that can't be solved by a good night's sleep." I patted the cold stone of the cave floor. "And no problem there—caves are known for their luxury accommodations, are they not?"

Instead of the sardonic quip or annoyed huff I expected, he tilted his head. "Liesel, do you ever feel as though you're not allowed to be sad? Or angry, or disappointed? To balance out your sister somehow?"

My pulse stuttered at the thoughtfulness—the insightfulness—of his question, but I doggedly ignored it. "Two uses of my name in a row, Breck. Dare I say our friendship can be declared official, in spite of your reluctance?"

"I mean it." He shifted to face me. "Your experiences today were far more than simply *trying*. If you're feeling scared or worried, you have every right to show it. There's no need to cover it with your quick wit and disarming grins." His voice softened as he leaned closer. "At least, not with me."

Nor with Me. The voiceless murmur caught me by surprise.

I know, Holy One. But He was already aware of my every thought and emotion. I couldn't hide if I wanted to. The people around me, on the other hand, would surely grumble or turn away if I proved too negative a burden.

Not the right ones.

I released a tremulous breath. The idea was tempting, but how could it be worth the risk to find out who wouldn't choose to distance themselves?

Shaking off unbidden tears, I returned Breck's expectant gaze. "I'm well. Though your concern is touching, and a definite sign that we're friends beyond just ornery guard and irritating princess. So at least something positive has come from our trials."

He continued to regard me with those intense amber eyes, until I couldn't look away.

I raised my hands. "Fine, yes. My parents are always concerned about Verena. I try not to add to their burden. But my very nature is mischievous and optimistic, so it doesn't require much effort. You know better than anyone that I cause plenty of trouble in my own way."

"Not *that* much trouble." Something almost resembling a smile crossed his face. "But please, Liesel. Tell me what's on your mind."

I pursed my lips. "That my guard is unusually pesky this evening?"

He huffed a sigh. "Then what were you thinking before I joined you?"

"Well, I—"

"Not the teasing version." He shook his finger at me like a scolding parent.

I opened my mouth to deflect once more, then paused. *Is this what You're nudging me toward, Holy One? Allowing Breck to see past the composure I'm trying so hard to maintain?*

But he had enough troubles of his own, and he already held me responsible for causing these problems myself...

Trust Me.

"Goodness, you are persistent." Both the Holy One and the determined man sitting before me. I glanced to where Nadette knitted something resembling a sock and Sir Jonas—who'd returned an hour before but had yet to say a word about his decision to continue on with us—tended the fire.

Leaning back against the cavern wall, I lowered my voice. "If you must know, I'm worried Sir Jonas won't be willing to come to Telynn Castle with us now that he knows the truth. That even if he does, he might not live up to what my sister remembers and she'll still be unhappy after all of this. I'm scared of what else Prince Carre or his men might try against me and my family." Shivering, I crossed my arms over my chest. "I'm embarrassed that I took on this foolish quest thinking I didn't need any protection. I feel—guilty, I guess, for dragging all of you into danger along with me." I glared past the tears blurring my vision. "Happy?"

"Yes, actually. Thank you for your honesty." He rested his arm on his raised knee. "I had my doubts about Jonas at first, but he's growing on me. I think he could be exactly what Princess Verena needs in a husband and future king." He scooted closer and placed a hand on my shoulder. "And you have no reason to plague yourself with guilt or shame. Your quest has a noble purpose. The approach may have been a bit foolhardy, but most of all I see your courage and loyalty and great love for your sister."

"You do?" My voice warbled like a toddler on the verge of a tantrum.

"I do." He shook his head. "I'm feeling my own humiliation that I thought my abilities were more than sufficient to protect you and Lady

Nadette on your journey. That I ever considered guarding the princess a paltry assignment."

I gave his fingers a squeeze. "You were so brave today, showing up exactly when I needed you. I'll be sure to let my father and Sir Ennoh know about your fine service. Hopefully it will earn you a promotion to a more interesting position."

"I don't want a different position." A new warmth in his eyes both drew me in and made me want to back away.

"Good." My whisper barely made a sound, but he seemed to understand. "If you hadn't been with us today, I would probably be his captive right now..." A shudder rippled down my back.

"You seemed to be holding your own well enough. But I will do everything in my power to keep you safe, Liesel." He shifted to lean against the cave wall at my side. The hand that had rested on my shoulder stretched out in invitation.

My breath fluttered in a quick, shallow rhythm. To lean against Breck, enter the warmth of his arms, sounded heavenly. But so vulnerable, to rest in his embrace by choice rather than necessity.

Yet he was inviting me in, even after I'd burdened him with my fears and woes. *Not that I should be surprised the Holy One was right.*

Before I could talk myself out of it, I closed the gap and tucked my head against his shoulder. Comfort and safety coursed through me as his arm circled my back, plus a hint of something more exhilarating I didn't dare dwell on. The fear and anxiety of the day finally melted away as I relaxed against the strength of his chest.

"Oh, dear. Princess Liesel, I'm not sure—" Nadette rose and headed toward us, twisting her fingers.

I stiffened. Innocent though it was, of course our embrace wouldn't be considered proper.

But Breck tightened his grasp, as though prepared to argue with my maid rather than relinquish his hold on me.

Sir Jonas appeared at Nadette's side and addressed her in murmured tones. I couldn't hear her response, but her frown softened as she nodded slowly. Looking back at us with a tight smile, she turned to her bedroll.

Hefting a quilt into his arms, Sir Jonas crossed the cavern and handed it to Breck. "We all need some rest after the scare today. Stay warm, and I'll keep the first watch."

Breck accepted the quilt, not seeming the least bit embarrassed about our embrace. "Thank you. I couldn't have saved Princess Liesel without you. I'll relieve you in a few hours."

Sir Jonas smiled his acknowledgment and returned to the fire, nearly tripping on a log as he got close.

"See? I told you I liked him." Breck tucked the quilt around us. "And he's right, let's get some sleep."

"Goodnight." I murmured into his shoulder.

I let my eyelids drift closed as he tipped his head against mine.

I awoke to quiet voices and rustling from the others packing up our few supplies. My neck ached from leaning against the hard stone wall, and shivers had replaced Breck's warmth in the cool morning air. A smile flitted across my lips, recalling the strange thrill of falling asleep in his arms again. I tightened my grip on the quilt. He must've tucked it closely around me whenever he'd risen to take over the night's watch.

Huffing out a half-groan, half-laugh, I released the quilt and pushed to my feet. *Just because Breck has come to my rescue more often than usual on this excursion doesn't mean I need to become a ninny about him.* But even with the chastisement running though my mind, a flock of hummingbirds seemed to awaken in my chest when Breck met my gaze with a lingering smile. *Snows, we need to get home as soon as possible.*

But were we even heading home?

As though summoned by the thought, Sir Jonas ducked into the cave. "Good morning, Princess Liesel." He waved, running his free hand over his damp hair.

"Good morning." I hurried to him, shuffling my feet to avoid tripping on the quilt draped over my arms. "I hope you were able to get some sleep."

"Enough." He gave an easy shrug. No amount of hardships—or difficult decisions—seemed capable of dimming the vibrancy of his grin. "We're all well and accounted for this morning, that's all I could ask."

"I couldn't agree more." I shifted the quilt to the crook of one arm. "Sir Jonas, I know it's completely unfair of me to rush you. Especially when it's my own fault you didn't know the true nature of our journey sooner, but—"

His eyes crinkled with mirth. "You'd like to know where we're heading this morning? Or at least which direction I plan to travel?"

A bit of the tension eased from my shoulders. "I confess I would. Though rest assured, I meant it when I said we'll accompany you back to Ormande if that's where you'd prefer to go."

Please, don't prefer to go back there.

"I appreciate the offer, Princess Liesel. But although your revelation last evening was certainly a shock, I haven't been able to stop thinking about your sister. Miserable enough that your father would invite any man to be his heir, simply because he could make her laugh. That you would travel all this way just because you remembered how I made Princess Verena smile." He dipped his head in a slow, decisive nod. "I have fond memories of your sister, and she was a beautiful girl. I can imagine, with the passing of years, that she has only..." He cleared his throat, rubbing the back of his neck. "That is to say, I would have no objection to marrying Princess Verena, if she would have me. And I can't stand the thought of abandoning her in her current state if there's something I can do to help."

A hiccup-shriek erupted from my throat as I launched myself at the wonderful man. "I knew it! I knew you would come for her once you heard."

Sir Jonas patted me gently on the back.

I released him and stepped away. "I apologize. Poor Nadette is going to have an apoplexy if I don't start reining in my unladylike behavior."

"Nothing unladylike in the least." He leaned forward in a conspiratorial whisper. "If all goes well, you and I will be brother and sister in no time."

Please, Holy One, let it be so.

Chapter 11

I tossed my embroidery aside at the sound of a trumpet blare. *Finally.* I'd returned two days before, eager for a bath and a comfortable bed.

And to avoid my family's questions about how my visit to Lady Ethelde had left me so disheveled.

Sir Jonas had paused in town for a stay at the inn, giving him time to prepare for what he would say to Verena and to hopefully allay suspicions about the timing of our arrivals. I'd seen Breck only in passing after he'd delivered our prisoner to Sir Ennoh. He'd been busy working with his fellow knights to bargain with the Unmasked Bandit for information, devise plans to anticipate Prince Carre's next move, and confiscate weapons from every Markan citizen who entered the castle gates. Breck's return to my silent, brooding guard—aside from a few extra smirks here and there—bothered me more than I cared to admit.

I'd been as flighty as a honeybee, flitting from one barely-noticed activity to the next as I awaited Sir Jonas's arrival. If this trumpet signaled another masked lackey of Prince Carre instead of Sir Jonas, I'd find a tomato to lob at him.

"Verena, come!" I paused at the door of the music room, where my sister put away the piece she'd been playing with all the speed of an island sloth.

It seemed her frown had become more permanent than ever during my absence. "I don't want to leave a mess."

"But you also don't want to keep your suitor waiting."

A puff of air escaped her lips, too defeated to be considered a laugh. "Don't I?"

I fiddled with the billowing sleeves of my deep purple dress as I waited, relishing the silky fabric after weeks of cotton.

Verena shuffled to the doorway, her emerald gown setting off her ivory complexion and dark hair. She presented a lovely, if not melancholy, picture. "All right. Let's see what this gentleman has to say."

I took her arm and dragged her along with me to the balcony. "Just think how nervous the poor fellow might be. Besides, now I'm here to suffer through the performances with you once again." I patted her hand. "Who knows, you might even like this one."

"I highly doubt..." We stepped out into the fresh air, and her words trailed off.

I bounced on my toes, barely holding back a squeal. In the courtyard stood Sir Jonas, clean-shaven, rested, and smiling with the warmth of the springtime sun. He'd exchanged his uniform from Lord Hamelun for a crisp tan tunic with a brown belt and trousers.

"Sir Jonas?" Verena's eyes widened in a mix of wonder and incredulity, her voice an awed whisper. "But how could he be here?"

"You're right, I think that is him." *Forgive my falsehood, Holy One.* I gave her arm a squeeze. "I told you he'd come if he ever found out about Pappa's proclamation."

Her head swiveled toward me, her brows lowering in suspicion. "So you did. But weren't you with—"

"Shh, he's getting started." *Good timing, Sir Jonas.* "You don't want to miss it."

Below, Sir Jonas spread his arms as the crowd quieted around him. "Princess Verena. You may not remember me, but I was a knight in service to your family years ago. In fact, I was the knight assigned to personally safeguard you for much of that time."

Verena nodded, her gaze riveted. As though he spoke to her alone instead of dozens of onlookers.

I silently thanked him for making it seem as though I hadn't revealed any hint of my sister's fondness for him.

"During that time, I enjoyed finding ways to make you smile or lighten your mood." His quavering voice gained in strength as he continued. "So today, I thought I'd reflect back on some of my antics. Especially the ones that went awry." He ducked his head with a sheepish grin.

A few good-natured chuckles echoed around the square.

Sir Jonas raised his hand. "But, before I begin, my good friend Sir Albrecht has graciously offered his assistance."

It was my turn to drop my jaw in astonishment. *Breck* had agreed to help him? The man who'd scoffed at the entire idea behind Pappa's proclamation?

Breck materialized from the crowd and took his place by Sir Jonas's side, sending a brief glance in my direction before turning his attention to the taller knight. At his feet, he set down some sort of squarish contraption covered in burlap. The contraption...rattled.

Even more curious than before, I scooted to the edge of my seat.

"Do you recall, Princess Verena, how you used to enjoy walks to the pond? A particularly fine goose there caught your eye, and I became determined to make a sort of pet of it." Raising his brows, he gestured to the shifting box.

With a dramatic flourish that made him hardly recognizable as my stoic guard, Breck lifted the burlap and unlatched a hook. The front of the crate released with a crash, setting free a white goose. The crowd alternately gasped and tittered, backing away to make room for the flailing, honking bird.

Sir Jonas scooped it up as though it were a wayward child. In return, the goose flapped a wing across his face and pecked at his hair. "But—like this one—the goose never took much of a liking to me." He ducked to protect his eyes from another flap.

I stole a glance at Verena, who shook her head with a hint of a smile. In the courtyard, Breck's shoulders quaked with suppressed laughter.

"It followed you around for some time, though, after you fed it all those crumbs from your pastry." Sir Jonas's words came out in short huffs as he danced from side to side, trying to keep his hold on the squirming goose. "That is, until the kitchen maid asked to pet the beautiful creature."

Verena winced as she leaned forward. Clearing his throat, Sir Jonas presented the goose to Breck.

Breck stretched his hand near enough to feign a pet, then lurched back with an unnaturally high shriek. "Get that creature away from here before I cook it for dinner!"

Tears pooled in the corners of my eyes at Breck's over-dramatic wail as he batted the goose away.

"Ah, well. We enjoyed it while it lasted." Sir Jonas released the bird with a sad droop of his head.

The crowd hastily cleared a path, but instead of embracing its new-found freedom, the goose honked and pushed its head against Sir Jonas's leg.

"Then there was the time..." Sir Jonas grunted against the persistent bird, trying to stand his ground. "The time I thought to impress you by kicking an old barrel to pieces but got my leg caught instead." With a quick step forward, he swung his other leg and caught his boot in the metal bars of the cage. Sir Jonas hopped, swatting at the goose who was pecking at the back of his knee.

Breck held out an arm for him to grasp as he lurched dangerously to one side, but Sir Jonas waved him away.

"What a sight I must've been, struggling against the barrel as I tottered this way and that like a newborn foal."

I swiped away an escaped tear as I peeked at Verena. Her chest rose and fell in quick huffs, as though suppressing laughter. *Keep going, Sir Jonas. You almost have her.*

"Perhaps I ought not recount this one, since it might get me in trouble with my fellow knights." Sir Jonas raised his voice above the onlookers' chuckles and the rattling cage that still clung to his foot. "But I once tried to sneak a weapon from the practice yard when you insisted you wanted to learn to wield a sword." He hobbled to the waist-high wall separating the outer courtyard.

Breck, who'd jogged ahead, handed him a large tongs.

Rising on tiptoe—especially precarious when the goose took a snap at his hip—Sir Jonas stretched the tongs over the wall.

"I had almost secured a wooden practice sword without detection, when the captain's dog sensed the attempted breach."

Leaning over the wall, Breck stretched his arms to reach something that must've been on the ground. A moment later, he resurfaced with a wriggling little dog. Casper, the feisty mutt belonging to our priest. Breck set him gently on the ground, and the dog barked with all his might, alternating between Sir Jonas, the metal cage, and the goose, as though unable to determine the most pressing threat.

The crowd's roars of laughter only made the dog bark more ferociously as Sir Jonas dragged the cage behind him in a fruitless attempt to flee. Seeming to realize they had a common foe, the goose tolerated the newcomer and snapped at Sir Jonas's hand.

Pursued by his odd little entourage and dragging the cage behind him, Sir Jonas hobbled back toward the center of the courtyard. Breck bent behind the short wall again to retrieve a bucket, then followed.

"It pains me to recall this last incident, though it did seem to amuse you the most of all my capers. Not that I intended for it to happen..." Sir Jonas winced as he walked on. "We'd ventured down to the fishing dock, if you recall, to see if I could procure some of your favorite walleye. But I know nothing of the ways of fishermen, and when one called out I didn't think to get out of the way. Or at least duck." He shook his head, his expression rueful. "So I got smacked in the face as an angler yanked a large catch onto the dock."

Breck reached into the bucket and lobbed something at Sir Jonas. It missed, sailing past him to flop on the pavement with a wet *splat*. A wide, silvery fish. A giggle bubbled in my chest as the crowd threw out good-natured taunts. The goose waddled away to inspect this new curiosity.

Narrowing his eyes in concentration, Breck removed another fish from the bucket and took aim, this time flicking the tail across Sir Jonas's cheek. The onlookers' cheers rose in volume when Sir Jonas caught the fish in one fist.

He inspected the fish with a shrug. "Unpleasant as a fish to the face may be, I must admit I'd take a fish over a goose any day." He lifted his head and gave Verena a bashful smile.

Hands gripping the railing, Verena bent at the waist, overcome by laughter.

I stiffened as Sir Jonas's eyes widened. Verena's giggles rang through the courtyard like a bell rusty from disuse.

She was laughing. *Verena* was *laughing*.

The crowd quieted, as though coming to the same realization. I glanced back to Sir Jonas, whose expression mixed awe with something like trepidation. His success would make him a betrothed man. The future king.

I squeezed an arm around Verena's waist as she straightened, swiping tears from her cheeks.

Tears stung my own eyes, springing from a source much deeper than mirth. "I've missed that sound."

She turned to me, her smile fragile but bright. "Me too." She stole another glance at the courtyard, where Sir Jonas stood motionless amidst a crowd buzzing with excitement. "I still can't believe he's here. You had something to do with it, didn't you?"

I patted her shoulder. "That's a story for another time. For now, you'd better see to your fiancé. His foot is still caught in that cage, after all, and there's no saying when the goose might return."

Her laughter flowed more naturally this time. "Good point." She moved toward the door, then turned back. "Thank you." Wrapping me in a hug, she buried her face in my shoulder.

I let the tears fall as I held her close. "It is *so* good to see you happy again."

The courtyard still hummed with excited murmurs when the guards threw open the doors for us.

"Sir Jonas." Verena advanced to where Breck was helping to extract his foot from the cage.

Sir Jonas adjusted his boot, then straightened. "Princess Verena." Their gazes latched, shy but thrumming with an undercurrent of anticipation.

"It's nice to see you back at Telynn Castle." I'd never heard Verena's voice so breathy, so animated. She glanced down at Sir Jonas's rumpled tunic and scuffed boots. "I do hope you didn't hurt yourself."

His face lit with a rueful smile. "No permanent injuries. At least, to anything but my pride."

She giggled, and his smile widened as he took a step closer.

I backed away to give them some privacy in their reunion. We'd done it. Sir Jonas was here, and he'd succeeded in making Verena laugh. Happiness and triumph blossomed in my chest, but less vibrant than I'd expected. I glanced back to where Sir Jonas now held Verena's fingers pressed in his, talking close to her ear.

Envy surged through my veins before I could rein it in. Verena would get her happy ending, married to her love. I was thrilled for her, and yet…

My gaze drifted to Breck, who was struggling to wrangle the bent bars of the cage back to their original shape. All at once, the happy ending I never realized I might want for myself felt entirely out of reach.

Swallowing a sigh, I pasted on a smile. I could hardly pine away for years at a time over a beloved guard the way Verena had. Now that we were back, life would return to normal. And I'd find a way to live it…somehow. Surely over time it would get easier.

I straightened my shoulders and spotted Casper. He'd been reunited with bald Father Lars, who was regaling anyone who would listen with the part his very own pup had contributed toward making the princess laugh. I obligingly gave the dog a pat for a job well done.

Nadette joined us, squeezing my elbow with a timid smile. She'd been hovering like a mother shadowlark over a nest of chicks ever since we'd returned. As though she suspected every castle guest harbored a plan to steal me away. Freed from the dirt and grime of our journey, her straw-colored hair shone in the sunlight. "You were right, milady. Sir Jonas was marvelous! Good gracious, I could scarcely believe…"

Her words faded as the guards opened the doors once more. From beneath the shadow of Verena's balcony, Pappa stepped out with a determined stride, linked arm in arm with Mamma, who wore a curious smile. They looked regal in shades of deep scarlet, a golden crown gleaming atop each of their heads.

The onlookers parted, finally quieting as every eye turned to the king and queen.

They stopped beside Verena, Pappa's eyes widening in surprised recognition when Sir Jonas straightened from his bow. "Sir...Jonas, was it?"

"Yes, Your Majesty." Sir Jonas gave a deferential nod. "It is good to be back at Telynn Castle once more."

"Indeed." Pappa held a whispered conversation with Sir Ennoh, who had appeared at his side.

I joined their circle next to Mamma, Nadette trailing behind. *Please accept Sir Jonas, Pappa. Please.*

Pappa gave a decisive nod, his smile wry but content. "It would seem, Sir Jonas, that you may be the only man in the kingdom who can make my daughter laugh. Therefore, I plan to fulfill my vow that Princess Verena's hand in marriage shall be yours, if you wish to accept it."

"Many thanks, Your Majesty. I am greatly honored by your praise and your generous offer." Jonas's flailing bow resembled a scarecrow buffeted by a strong wind. "But I'm afraid I did not work alone to make the princess laugh. Sir Albrecht made an equally valuable contribution." He pulled a bewildered Breck to his side.

A new wave of whispers simmered through the crowd. Verena stepped back, appearing confused and a bit hurt, and Pappa blinked his eyes in rapid succession.

I pressed my lips together, holding back the protest clawing at my throat. *What are you doing, you fool? Our plan worked—hurry up and accept the marriage offer before Pappa changes his mind.*

Nadette caught my eye, her expression almost more amused than concerned. Had Sir Jonas shared something about this with her? If only we could escape the curious gazes of the many spectators so I could ask.

Pappa choked out what he likely meant to be a chuckle and lowered his voice. "I appreciate your sense of justice, Sir Jonas, but you were certainly the main performer in this effort to amuse the princess. And presumably the instigator. You can hardly suggest that she marry two men. Therefore, it seems only fitting that you marry Princess Verena, unless this young man objects..."

He gestured to Breck, who shook his head with wide eyes.

I bit back a grin. Verena and Breck would make a terrible match, his stodginess only adding to her natural solemnity.

Sir Jonas held his head high. "Certainly Princess Verena could hardly marry two gentlemen, Your Majesty. Yet it would be the height of injustice to allow me to claim such a priceless treasure as your daughter while Sir Albrecht, though equally deserving, walks away empty-handed."

My face scrunched into a wince before I could stop it. Sweet and earnest, Sir Jonas may be, but the man clearly lacked the ability to follow the simplest of instructions.

Pappa rubbed his forehead with a sigh, turning to Breck. "Would a monetary reward suit you? Perhaps the deed to a property?"

Breck spread his hands. "I only intended to help a friend, Your Majesty. There's no need—"

Sir Jonas raised a finger and lifted his brows. "Forgive my interruption, Your Majesty. But may I point out that you have a second princess?"

Chapter 12

"A second princess?" Though Pappa gaped at him, Sir Jonas appeared as though he were adding an interesting counterpoint to an academic debate rather than suggesting the King of Walthar marry off his other daughter.

His other daughter... *Me.* My gaze flew to Breck, then to the ground, then to the trees at the far end of the courtyard. Heat seared my cheeks, but I could hardly draw further attention by cooling them with my clammy palms. Sir Jonas was trying to convince Pappa to give my hand in marriage to Breck. But did he want that?

Did I want that?

My gaze returned to Breck. The scruff he never seemed to be able to shave cleanly off his jaw. The ironic tilt of his mouth that every once in a while broadened into the brightest of grins. His arms that enclosed me in such safety and warmth. His deep amber eyes that lit with such intelligence and humor.

Yes, I wanted to marry him very much. The answer sang from the depths of my being, where I'd attempted to keep it suppressed for days.

It seemed I should be giving Sir Jonas another hug rather than scolding him.

A glance at Pappa showed his consternation at this turn of events. If the turning heads were any indication, no one could decide whether to watch him, Sir Jonas, Breck, Verena, or me.

Steeling myself with the deepest breath my stays would allow, I stepped forward. "What an interesting solution you propose, Sir Jonas. It seems your creative thinking extends far beyond your ability to keep my sister entertained—a trait that will serve you well in the royal family."

Sir Jonas turned to me with a wide smile. "I hope you're right, Princess Liesel." His brows lifted in clear expectation. "Don't you agree it would be unjust to allow Sir Albrecht to walk away with something so paltry as a property deed?"

My racing heart seemed determined to clog my throat. "I..."

Pappa leaned forward, his flustered expression bordering on panic. Mamma regarded me with a mix of sympathy and interest, while Verena's soft eyes radiated a hopeful, almost teasing glint. Nadette squirmed, her thumbs tracing the edges of her apron. Her tight smile seemed torn between amusement and a desire to protest the impropriety of Sir Jonas's suggestion.

When I'd run out of other faces to study, I reluctantly raised my eyes to Breck. His skin was paler than I'd ever seen it, and he didn't seem to be breathing. His guarded expression searched my face for an answer, but which one? Did he want me to release him from Sir Jonas's crazy plan, or—? The alternative seemed too wonderful and preposterous to put into words.

Breck cleared his throat. "If you'd permit me, Your Majesty, might I speak with Princess Liesel in private? I believe Sir Jonas's proposition has come as a surprise to both of us."

A word in private. *Yes. Good—maybe?*

Pappa regarded him with narrowed eyes. "You may, but not beyond our line of sight."

Color returned to Breck's cheeks as he lowered into a brief bow. "Of course, Your Majesty."

Unwilling to meet any of the inquisitive gazes that trailed our every movement, I followed Breck out of our haphazard ring, beyond crowds of milling people, to a comparatively open space on the patio.

Say something, Liesel. Anything. "How—how is your father? Have you had a chance to visit him yet?"

"My...father?" Breck blinked at me in confusion.

"Yes. You said he was ill, remember? On Siebennet, when we prayed."

"Ah, yes. I saw him yesterday. If anything, he seemed a bit improved since before our journey."

"I'm very glad to hear it." We stopped walking, and the curious scrutiny of so many villagers brought a wave of heat up my neck.

"Thank you. But Liesel—" Breck gripped my arm, looked down at his hand, and quickly released me. "I apologize for this...confusion, and any embarrassment or scandal it may cause. I had no idea Jonas would make that ludicrous suggestion. Hopefully you know that I only helped him to secure his happiness with your sister. And because I wanted your plan to succeed." His voice softened, almost to the point of timidity.

"That was my assumption. There's no need to apologize." My laugh held only a fragile remnant of its usual mirth. "Sir Jonas is anything but predictable."

"That he is." He ran his hand through his hair, giving a yank when he caught on a snarl. "Please feel no obligation, or fear that..." He straightened his shoulders. "I will always serve you and your family, Liesel. Always protect you with my life. As your guard, and as your—friend. I'm not going anywhere. I want you to know that you won't anger me or lose anything by refusing Jonas's proposal." He glanced up with raised brows, the quirk of his lips failing to produce the teasing smile he likely intended. "Unless, of course, you *want* to marry me." His gaze transferred back to the ground, where his boot scuffed at a divot in the stone.

He was giving me an escape. A chance to say *We'd kill each other,* or *I could never marry someone who doesn't like roasted apples* in a lighthearted way that would leave our hearts and prides relatively intact.

But would it? Would my heart ever truly recover from our adventure together? From the experience of being seen, being rescued, being held, by this clever, brave, caring, frustrating man? My mouth opened, but I couldn't push any words out.

Safe as a bantering retreat might be, I couldn't force myself to take it.

As the silence stretched on, Breck raised his head. "Liesel?" The longing in his questioning gaze nearly drew me a step forward.

At least, I hoped it was longing.

He took a step toward me, apparently drawn by the same inexplicable tug. "Do you want to marry me?" The question released on a whisper for my ears alone.

Troublesome tears filled my eyes as I stared into those amber depths. My throat dry as a desert, I could only nod.

His breath released in a half-laugh, half-sob. He raised his hands as if to cup my face, then blinked and dropped to his knees. He took my hands in his, gripping them so tightly I couldn't tell which one of us was trembling. "I have nothing to offer you, Liesel. You know I'm working my way up the ranks as a knight with little to my name. I'm too gruff to impress anyone—especially royalty—or to sweep you off your feet the way you deserve. But I do love you. Everything I have, everything I am is entirely yours. That is, if you want it."

"Stand up before you make a scene." With a watery giggle, I tugged him to his feet. "I don't know how Sir Jonas knew, but of course I want to marry you. My irritating, wonderful guard I can't seem to live without." Releasing his hands, I slid my palms to his shoulders. "Everything you are is more than enough for me."

His eyes roamed my face, as though needing one last confirmation that I meant what I said. Then he hugged me against his chest, his fingers tangling in my hair, his lips finding mine in a caress both gentle and fervent.

A throat cleared behind us, followed by a cough. My mind refused to be distracted from the delirium of Breck's kiss, until a finger poked my arm. "Liesel, Sir Albrecht." Verena whispered beside my left ear.

With an internal gasp, I remembered the crowds—*my parents*—and leaned back from Breck. He loosened his embrace, but kept an arm looped around my waist.

Verena regarded me with pink cheeks and eyes wide with shock and...humor? "You've found your happiness, too." Her smile seemed uncertain, but genuine.

"It seems I have." I took the opportunity to wipe the tears from my cheeks. "Thanks to your Sir Jonas."

Pappa stepped forward with a huff. "May I assume the two of you are planning to be married?" He passed a glance full of meaning—not to mention warning—between myself and Breck.

"Yes, Pappa." I pushed a loose curl behind my ear. "I apologize we got a bit...carried away."

Nadette's reproving head shake was undermined by her soft smile and tear-filled eyes.

Breck squared his shoulders. "It would be my great honor to marry your daughter, Your Majesty. Since she doesn't object to me as her groom."

"Clearly not." Pappa's expression relaxed into a rueful smile. "Both of my daughters marrying their guards."

"Marryin' the men they love." Mamma leaned her head against his arm, taking his hand in both of hers.

He shook his head. "At least you ought to be well protected."

"That they shall." Sir Jonas strode to Verena's side. "Ouch." His attempt at brandishing his dagger ended with the point catching on the belt of his tunic. "By Sir Albrecht, at least." He tucked the blade away with a sheepish smile.

Verena's giggle bubbled up like a fountain re-animated in the first warmth of spring. Tucked against Breck's side, I reached and gave her hand a squeeze.

Pappa's chuckle added a baritone harmony beneath her soprano as he patted Sir Jonas on the back. "You'll have plenty of knights for that task, my boy. Other concerns will keep you plenty busy, if you're to become king one day."

Verena looked up at her fiancé with shining eyes. "What a dedicated, compassionate king he'll be."

I couldn't agree more.

Verena played a lively fugue on the pianoforte in our sitting room after dinner that evening. When had she learned anything other than her solemn dirges over the past seven years?

Sir Jonas could hardly keep his eyes off her from where he sat on a divan, admiration lighting his face. Breck and I sat across from him, our hands clasped as they'd been practically all evening.

I traced my thumb across Breck's calloused knuckles, tilting my head to study my soon-to-be brother-in-law. "Jonas, I have to ask. What inspired you to include Breck in your negotiations with my father? He claims he wasn't in on your plan."

I nudged Breck, who shrugged with a look of exaggerated innocence.

Jonas grinned. "He tells the truth, Princess Liesel." He rubbed his hands along the thick fabric of his trousers. "I've never been an admirable knight when it comes to physical strength or coordination, but we're also taught to be observant. To pay attention to details that could point to a person's true motives, in order to anticipate surprise attacks." His gaze warmed with humor. "In this case, it didn't take me long to pick up on certain signs of attraction between the two of you."

At my side, Breck leaned forward with interest.

Jonas gestured toward him. "Albrecht's gaze follows you wherever you go, Princess Liesel. At least when he thinks you're not looking. Far beyond what's needed for your protection. And despite his assertions that you're fickle or impossible to please, he does a remarkable job of anticipating your desires. The clear mark of a man who's been studying a lady and wants to take charge of her future happiness."

Breck's neck shrank into his shoulders when I glanced his way. I placed a playful kiss on his warm cheek.

His mock glare failed to reach his eyes. "What about her? I doubt you would've made the attempt if you thought I was doomed to suffer a refusal."

"Certainly not." Jonas balanced his elbows on his knees. "Princess Liesel smiles more in your company than anyone else's."

I jabbed Breck's arm. "Only because I take such pleasure in teasing him."

Jonas continued, unfazed. "And she seems to look for any excuse to be in physical contact with you—taking your arm, shoving your chest, huddling close."

My mouth opened in an incoherent protest.

Breck's hearty laugh shook the settee. "Notice he speaks in present tense." He bent close, until his breath tickled my ear. "But let me assure you, I'm enjoying every moment." The teasing glint in his eyes deepened to something much more poignant.

My stomach twisted into a knot of anticipation.

"Dance with me?" He rose and held out a hand.

I blinked in a pitiful attempt to clear my head. Verena's melody had shifted to a slow, pensive waltz. "Happily. But I didn't realize you were fond of dancing."

"I haven't been, until this precise moment." He pulled me as close as the dance steps allowed. "But if you're looking for excuses to be near me, I'll gladly provide every opportunity."

I shook my head, releasing a huff. "Careful, or I might *accidentally* stomp on your toes."

He circled an arm around my waist, his gaze brimming with mischief. "I'll take my chances."

"When are you going to explain how you and Sir Albrecht seem to know Jonas so well already? And why he happened to appear only days after you returned from your unusually long trip?" Verena took my arm as we strolled through the sprawling gardens behind the castle. Lilacs scented the air while bright daffodils and tulips nodded in the afternoon sunshine.

I couldn't contain my impish grin. "Let's just say, my trip took a detour in the direction of Ormande. A beautiful, if not isolated, part of our fine kingdom."

That I hoped to never see again.

"Jonas and I would like to travel there after we're married so he can bid a proper farewell to everyone he got to know during his years with Lord

Hamelun." Her steps paused. "But, Liesel, did you truly travel all that way just for me? Wasn't it terribly dangerous, especially without a sled or a proper set of guards?"

Self-consciousness heated my cheeks. "Breck kept me safe enough."

"It seems he did." Her hint of a teasing smile seemed so foreign and yet infinitely lovely. "But even with him along, it was quite reckless of you. Jonas tells me the mountain passages that far north can be treacherous."

"We encountered a few challenges along the way." No need to scare my protective older sister—or earn myself a lecture—with details of damaged supplies, rockslides, missing elk, and kidnapping attempts. "Just enough to make it feel like an adventure."

"And to bring you close to the guard you claimed to dislike."

"That, too." I cleared my throat and patted her hand. "But I would've gone through far worse terrain, endured any discomfort, if it meant seeing you this happy." I stepped ahead to face her. "This is what you want now, right? You don't feel obligated because Jonas came all this way? You're not forcing smiles because you suspected I went through an ordeal to bring Jonas to you?"

"Nothing of the sort." A full-fledged smile bloomed across her face, every bit as bright and beautiful as the blossoming flowers surrounding us. "How could anyone not laugh with Jonas around? He is such a good man and cares for me in a way I don't think anyone else ever could. I'm so very grateful." She tugged my arm to continue walking. "I'd ask you similar questions, except no one who sees you and Sir Albrecht together could doubt you're in love."

My mouth opened and closed a few times, my tongue suddenly dry. *Is it that obvious?* "Well, I certainly..."

"Don't even attempt to deny it, my love."

I jumped at Breck's soft voice and Jonas's good-natured chuckle on the path behind us.

Jonas strode between us and claimed Verena's arm. "Sorry to interrupt your walk, but we simply couldn't go another minute without our lovely fiancées."

"It's quite true." Breck put a hand on my lower back, steering me in the opposite direction of Jonas and Verena. "I'm afraid I'm every bit as besotted with you, dear Liesel, as you are with me."

I snorted but waved to Verena and Jonas and allowed Breck to lead me down a smaller side path. Twining my arm with his, I gazed up at him. "Your affection isn't starting to wane now that we're back at the castle? Now that you're surrounded by memories of the many times I've irritated you and a multitude of options for company, including other fair young ladies?"

"Are there other fair young ladies at the castle? I hadn't noticed." He tugged me closer to his side. "None of them could compare with your adventurous spirit or fierce care for your loved ones, even if they might get into slightly less trouble."

"Only slightly, hmm?" I slid my fingers down his arm to clasp his hand. "Does your presence here in the gardens mean the investigation is complete?"

"Yes." He linked our fingers. "It seems your Unmasked Bandit truly was acting without the knowledge or consent of the Markan royal family. His stay in the dungeons will last for some time."

I held back a shudder. The odious man deserved every moment in that foul place. "And Prince Carre?"

Breck shrugged. "We'll keep a close eye on him, of course. But for the moment, he seems deflated by his failure to secure a marriage alliance and embarrassed that his servant took such drastic steps. I believe we have reason to hope everything will be quiet on that front, at least for now."

My relief escaped in a contented sigh. We walked on, the warm sunshine, vibrant garden, Breck's affection, and Verena's newfound happiness nearly overwhelming me with a surge of joy.

"Liesel?" Breck traced his thumb across my palm. "Is something wrong?"

"Not in the least." I laughed, even as tears clogged my throat. "I just can't believe we did it. Verena and Jonas… We got him here, and after all my evasiveness, he actually *wanted* to marry Verena. She's happier than I've ever seen her. The threat from Markou is past. And I—" I sniffed, forcing myself to meet the intensity of his amber eyes. "I wasn't even looking for… I didn't think anyone who got a glimpse of my fear or sadness, anything negative I tried to hide, could ever…" I swallowed. *Time to complete a sentence, Liesel.* "I doubted anyone existed who could want *all* of me, and I certainly wasn't on the lookout for him."

"I know exactly what you mean." His tone was so soft, yet thrumming with emotion.

"It turns out he was right here all along." I stepped closer, moving my hands to his shoulders.

"I'm so grateful we both finally saw it." He cupped my cheek, placing the gentlest of kisses on my forehead, then my lips.

"Me too." I toyed with a curl of hair that peeked beneath his ear. "But will you still love me if I rescue another bird, do you think?"

His quiet chuckle vibrated in his chest. "I think I'll manage."

"When I sneak off for a nighttime ride?"

His mouth quirked to one side. "Only if you invite me to join you."

"What about—?"

"Liesel." He brought a finger to my lips. "I'm sure I'll get irritated with you on occasion, as you will with me. But that will never change how much I care for you."

Tears threatened again. *Thank You, Holy One. For leading me to a man who can love me in spite of—maybe even because of—my wild schemes. For forcing me to look past his gruff exterior to his beautiful heart. For knowing everything I try to hide and still embracing me as Your daughter.*

Swallowing, I batted my eyelashes at him with a grin. "I'm glad to hear it. Though at least now I have a much more effective method of quelling your irritation."

He lowered a brow, his voice teasing. "Oh? And what's that?"

I rose to my toes, channeling all my gratitude and love into a thorough kiss.

CORNERSTONE SERIES

A Noble Purpose
Laurie Lucking

A Noble Past
Anna Augustine

A Noble Match
Kirsten Fichter

A Noble Warrior
Lucy Peterson

A Noble Grace
E.G. Bella

A Noble Loyalty
Olivia Godfrey

A Noble Heart
Jewell Windall

A Noble Intent
Kendall Hoxsey

A Noble Princess
Saraina Whitney

A Noble Rescuer
K.R. Mattson

A Noble Companion
Rachel Kovaciny

A Noble Life
C.K. Heartwing

A Noble Assassin
Abigail Kay Harris

A Noble Friend
Kendra E. Ardnek

A Noble Protector
Madisyn Carlin

A Noble Comfort
Katja H. Labonté

LEARN MORE AT WWW.BEYONDTHEBOOKERY.COM

As the little sister to the crown prince, Miette was never meant to be in a position of prestige and power. And she was content to remain that way. Maintaining her butterflies is a much easier task than ruling a kingdom, after all. The butterflies don't pressure her to make hard decisions and accept a husband from an approved list of suitors.

But when Miette's brother dies, the kingdom of Barlencoy becomes her most unwelcome gift. The land is torn apart by the classes, and rebellion boils at her doorstep. War is looming, and no one seems afraid of it. The kingdom may be hers, but she has no voice to quieten the tremors that threaten to tear everything she knows and loves apart.

Gavin Vollo is a guard without a purpose. Moving forward after the death of the crown prince, his best friend, has been no easy task. Especially when the prince's death is Gavin's own fault. He'll never understand why the prince had to die – just like he'll never understand why the royal force wants him back to guard the new queen.

Available October 8th, 2024 – preorder now!
https://www.amazon.com/gp/product/B0CRH3LN6H

Acknowledgements

The Cornerstone Series has been such a delight to work on! Many thanks to Abigail for leading the project and inviting me to join, Madisyn for her gorgeous cover designs (through Mountain Peak Edits & Design) and invaluable guidance, and every member of the group who provided advice, encouragement, or a dose of humor. It's been an honor to collaborate with you ladies, and I can't wait to see what's coming next on your writing journeys!

I had such a fabulous team of beta readers for *A Noble Purpose*! Laura, Brianna, Marilyn, Renuka, and Ms. Z-K – you each provided that perfect combination of insightful comments and enthusiasm for my story that gave me renewed energy to enter into editing mode. This book has so many more important details (and less inconsistencies!) thanks to all of you!

Elise – I'm so fortunate to call you a friend and to gush about our favorite books together. And I couldn't ask for a better proofreader! Thank you so much for using your talents to help get this story ready for publication, your support for me and my writing means so much.

My family continues to be unfailingly supportive in all the ups and downs of my author journey, including when I signed up to write two books within one year! Your love and encouragement give me the freedom to keep dreaming up new stories and bringing them to life. I love you all more than I can express!

And as always, I'm so grateful to God for inspiring me with stories and opportunities to reach readers, and to YOU for taking the time to read my book! Nothing makes me feel more fulfilled than writing a story that brightens a reader's day and then hearing about how it touched them. Thank you for being one of those readers.

Also by Laurie Lucking

Tales of the Mystics

Common

Traitor (coming in 2025)

The Intertwined Tales

The Dancer and the Dragon Speaker (coming Dec. 6, 2024)

Read on for a sneak peek!

The Dancer and the Dragon Speaker

SNEAK PEEK

CHAPTER I

"Will someone fix my hair?" My sister Rosalind's whisper made the candle on her vanity flicker.

"In a minute." I tied the wide pink ribbon around my youngest sister's waist into a bow at the back. "All done, Pippa."

She craned her neck and smiled as I patted her shoulder. "Danil says he doesn't like pink, but it's still my favorite color."

With an effort, I kept my jaw unclenched. "You don't need to worry about what Danil thinks. You look lovely."

"But I do want him to think I'm pretty." Pippa swished her silk skirt with a flourish. "He's the only one I ever get to dance with."

"Only for now." Rose and I shared an uneasy look in the mirror as I crossed the room to where she sat on a cushioned stool. "Next year, you'll finally get to attend balls and parties here in Oneska. Then I'm sure you'll have dozens of dance partners."

"Not as many as Rose, I bet." At age twelve, Pippa hated being left behind with a governess while the rest of us attended social events. She twirled, then sank onto the edge of her bed.

Rose didn't manage to hide a self-satisfied smirk. "Even I don't *always* fill my dance card."

I stifled a huff. Universally acknowledged as the most beautiful of the five Oneskan princesses, a failure to fill her dance card only meant Rosalind was choosing to be coy. I pushed a jeweled pin into her hair to hold a braid in place.

Callista, two years older than Rose, faced Pippa with a smile. "We'd all have sore feet if we danced as much as Rose. Besides, with your long curls, blue eyes, and quick wit you're sure to attract many suitors once you're old enough." She fastened a string of pearls around her neck and sat next to Pippa.

I glanced at my own reflection as I swept more of Rose's lustrous dark curls atop her head. Straight, unremarkable hair, pale skin, lips pressed into a thin line, eyes lined with worry. No doubt the only reason any gentleman ever asked me to dance was due to my status as the Crown Princess.

"Ouch!" Rose rubbed at her head where I'd been inserting another pin. "Careful with those."

"Sorry." Shaking my head in an attempt to focus my thoughts, I slowly slid the pin into her hair. Tonight I needed to protect my sisters, not fret about my appearance.

"If only we didn't have to change into our nightclothes and get re-dressed every time." Rose heaved a dramatic sigh.

Calli gave a sympathetic nod. "It would be much easier if we could at least get help from our maids."

"But that would make them suspicious, right?" Pippa bounced on the edge of her bed.

"Exactly." Calli patted her knee, then glanced around. "Jolene, did you still need help with—?"

"Jo!" Pippa's scolding tone drowned out Calli's question. "You aren't even dressed yet!"

Jolene, our second-youngest sister, sank further into the cushions on her bed. "Why do I have to go? There aren't even enough princes, and Pippa enjoys it more."

"Speaking of not making anyone suspicious..." I gave Pippa a quelling look. "We have to keep it quiet in here. And Jo, we've been through this. Prince Leonnar has requested that all five of us be in attendance. You know we can't afford to...anger him."

Calli hurried across the room to her. "We're all tired, dear one. But it's not so bad. Maybe they'll have some of those honey cakes you like so much." Putting an arm around Jo's shoulders, Calli helped her slide off the bed.

"But why do we have to work so hard to look nice? We don't even like them." Jo crossed her arms over her chest with a glower only a four-teen-year-old could achieve.

Rose snorted, and I covered a laugh of my own before turning around. "We're still representatives of Oneska, even in places or situations we'd rather avoid. And you'd best hurry, we don't want our *escorts* to get restless."

Rose shuddered, all traces of humor gone. "I can finish up my hair, thank you Emelia."

I gave her a quick nod before joining Calli in pulling a dress over our reluctant sister's head.

Want to find out what happens next? *The Dancer and the Dragon Speaker* entwines The Twelve Dancing Princesses with The Language of the Birds to create one new happily-ever-after. Preorder today! https://www.amazon.com/Dancer-Dragon-Speaker-Laurie-Lucking-ebook/dp/B0D6PQCR9F/

Reviews

Thanks so much for taking the time to read *A Noble Purpose*! If you enjoyed this adventure, please consider leaving a review on Amazon or sharing about it on social media.

Even a sentence or two will help more readers discover Princess Liesel's story. Thank you!!

About the Author

Laurie Lucking loves books, music, and spending time with her family in beautiful Minnesota. A recovering attorney, she now spends her days chasing her active 2-year-old, answering hundreds of questions for her preschooler, and struggling through her sons' math homework (plus a little cooking and cleaning when absolutely necessary). When she finds a spare moment, she writes young adult romantic fantasy inspired by fairy tales.

Laurie's novels have won the Excellence in Editing Award and finaled in the Carol Awards. Her short stories have been published in Deep Magic e-zine, Brio magazine, and a number of anthologies. She enjoys connecting with readers through her website, www.laurielucking.com (sign up for her newsletter to receive a free short story!), and in the Facebook group she co-founded, Faith and Fairy Tales.

www.ingramcontent.com/pod-product-compliance
Lightning Source LLC
Chambersburg PA
CBHW060332310726

48976CB00007B/2528